My King

A Stalker Romance
In The Shadows Series
Book 2

By Dahlia Dempsey

Copyright © 2025 Dahlia Dempsey

All rights reserved.

This is a work of fiction. Similarities to real people, places, or events are entirely coincidental.

No part of this book may be reproduced, or stored in a retrieval system, or transformed in any way without the permission of the author.

First edition. May 1, 2025.

ISBN: 9798282872644

Written by Dahlia Dempsey

PA: Britney Oliver

CONTENT WARNING

This book is not suited for people under the age of 18 as it contains language, sexual encounters, and mature scenes.

Trigger Warning

Stalking.

Murder.

Womanizer.

My King is the second of four books of a stalker romance series, In The Shadows Series.

Dedication

To all the "ordinary" women out there looking for more, looking to be seduced. You have come to the right place. Now do as you're told, Princess.

My King

A Stalker Romance
In The Shadows Series
Book 2

By Dahlia Dempsey

Prologue

Before her, there was only emptiness…and the occasional body. I've been searching for her between the women. I exist for one reason: to find her. And that's exactly what I plan to do.

I walked around, actively trying to fill this void. I treat life as if it were an instruction manual.

1. Get up
2. Take a shower
3. Work
4. Eat
5. Workout
6. Fuck
7. Sleep
8. Search for her

That's how my life went until I met her. But then I saw her. After that, I was magnetized. I thought I was interested in other women, but she was nothing compared to my one.

I can't bring myself to confront her just yet. I don't want to ruin anything. I need to wait for the perfect time to make my presence known. She needs to be ready for me, and I need to get rid of Rachel first. She will only get in the way.

I've been searching for her since before my first murder. One by one, I've been ridding this world of the true lowlifes for her. Now that I have found her, I'll never let her out of my sight. I'll never let her go. She will be mine, even if I have to end everyone that gets in my way. I'll never let her go. She will be mine, and I'll kill every last motherfucker that gets in my way. I'll burn this world to the ground if I have to. I'll even take myself down with it.

I've been patient long enough. Tonight, I make my move.

Before her.....

Chapter 1 Conrad

I watch as the long legged blonde slowly approaches me. I knew she would, they always do. It's like a moth drawn to a flame. They can't help themselves. It's inevitable. No point in fighting it. I'm not being cocky. I'm just being truthful. The gods blessed me with a face and body from above. Why would I not use it to my advantage?

I stopped at the usual place after work. I don't have the time to find another usual spot. This place will do for now. I only come here when I need to get my dick wet, and it's been one of those weeks. The kind of week where only a pussy can solve. The girls know me here. I try not to fuck the same one more than a handful of times. They start to get needy after that, and I'm not interested in that. Not with them at least.

There are plenty of options here. Blondes. Brunettes. Red heads. Big tits. Little tits. Tall. Short. Everything. The only issue is I haven't found *the one*. I've found several ones, but not *the one*. Every time I find a prospect, I just end up getting disappointed. It's starting to annoy the fuck out of me. I know she's out there. It's as if I can feel she is close. There has to be one girl out there that is worth it all.

I have to shake my thoughts away about my one because she isn't here for me to own yet. The blonde sure as hell ain't the one, but she will do for tonight. She has on a black fitted dress that barely comes down to cover her voluptuous ass. I can't help but wonder how she'll feel under my touch. Will she feel…right? Will she feel….wrong? My dick gets excited about the thought of diving into her. I'll know soon enough if she's worth my time.

"Hey sexy. Buy me a drink?" She says in a way that I'm not sure if it's a question or not. I nod to the bartender to grab another round for the lady. I don't need another drink. I don't plan to be here for long. The only thing I'm debating is if I want to take the time to drive to her place or fuck her in the bathroom? There's also a nice spot out back. Two walls that come together making a nice corner I can shove them against.

This one looks like she'd be perfectly fine with being shoved up against the wall in the back alley. As soon as the bartender hands her the drink, she looks up at me and smiles. "Thank you. That was nice of you," she says, as if she didn't just insist I buy her one.

Thankfully, since I was old enough to work on my own, I haven't had to worry about money. My dad was a decent man. He worked hard and built his own empire, my empire. I run a very successful financial firm. Sure, my father built it, but when I took it over after he passed, it soared.

My mother on the other hand, well there aren't any polite words I could use to describe her. She left when I was a young teenager, basically didn't want to be a mother anymore. Bitch.

I will admit, I changed the day she left. The day she told me I wasn't worth sticking around for. Fucking bitch. But I think I changed for the better. I'm more aware of the world. I know my purpose in life, and that is to find the one.

The one I can count on to never leave me. The one I can trust with my life. The one I can hold onto and never let go. The one that I can possess. The one that I will put a baby in and raise that kid right.

Again, I have to push the thoughts out of my head. I nod to the blonde. I watch her as she slowly drinks the mixed drink I ordered for her. "Bathroom or alley?" I lean over and whisper in her ear. She lets out a small giggle. "What kind of girl do you think I am?" she reaches over and plays with my finger that is gripping my drink.

"The kind that wants her pussy to be drenched and legs shaking after I'm done with her." I watch as she registers everything I just said. Her little brown eyes widened in response. It's not lost on me that she hasn't said no or pulled away from me. Tired of waiting, I make the decision for her. I grab her hand and pull her with me. She's right on my tail as I shove the back door open and push her against the wall.

I don't wait for the blonde to protest. I slam my lips against hers and have my way with her. I don't want to hear her talk because her voice is too nasally for my liking.

Closing my eyes, I picture what my one would look like. I always see brown hair and hazel eyes. She's small, but not too small. As I grab the blonde's tits, I think about what my girl's boobs would feel like. They would be small but not too small. They would be just right to fit in my hands.

The blonde moans as I pinch her nipple above her dress. I can't help, but think of what my girl would sound like. I know her voice will be soft and sweet and eager at my touch.

I slide my hand between her thighs and quickly dip my hand into her underwear. She's already wet, which means she wants this as quickly as I do. I don't waste any time unzipping my slacks and pulling out my hardening dick.

Reaching into my pocket, I pull out a much needed condom and slide it over myself. She watches me with lustful eyes. "Turn around," I say to her. She willingly does exactly as I say. Greedy whore. Makes it easier for me. I don't waste any time sliding my dick into her and tearing up her wet pussy. Pulling on her hair so I can control the movement better I hear her scream. I'm not sure if it's from pleasure or pain, but I don't care. All I can think about is getting off to the image of my girl taking my dick. I keep my eyes closed because every time I see this blond hair, it ruins the mood.

I feel the blonde tighten around me and she comes hard. The feeling of her milking me makes me want to get off even faster. I pick up the pace as I continue to slam into her regardless of the word she's mumbling. Just as I am about to explode I hear the back door, but I ignore everything else. I can feel eyes on me, which only makes me pound harder. What can I say? I like an audience.

Just as I find my release, I look over and see a sexy little brown haired woman watching me with heat in her eyes. She doesn't shy away. She watches me get off inside of another woman, and fuck if that isn't hot.

Most women would have shied away. I have to admit, I'm intrigued. "Did you enjoy the show?" I ask the woman, completely ignoring the blonde that is still bent over. My dick is still inside of her as I flirt with the sexy, hazel eyed woman.

I pull out and discard the condom in the dumpster nearby. The hazel eyed woman watches my every move. Her eyes haven't stopped watching my dick. As her eyes slowly drift up to meet my eyes, I smile. Unable to help it, I start to get hard once again.

"It could use some work, but the technique seemed to work for her." Did she just imply my technique wouldn't work for her? My technique works for every-fucking-one. Even though she just insulted me, I can't help but grin at the size of her balls.

"Would you like to come over here and let me show you my technique and prove you wrong?" The blonde woman pulls down her dress and slaps me across the face. "Asshole." She walks back inside completely, ignoring the woman that I have not taken my eyes off, despite the slap to the face.

"I'm good, thanks. I don't like sloppy seconds. But I'm sure if you hurry you could grab your blonde friend back. She seems just about as smart as that dumpster over there. I'm sure she will forget all about the fact that you're flirting with me while your dick was still inside of her." I can't help but laugh at her wit.

Filling my dick grow harder I decide it's time to put it back inside my slacks. "Oh, is the fun over?" She puts her hand on her hip and sticks out her bottom lip as she pouts.

"Hey, you're the one that said you didn't want sloppy seconds." I walk over to her and reach for the door knob. "But baby, with me ain't nothing sloppy about it. I'd have you on your knees begging for more. That's a promise."

I can tell she's a little stunned by my words so I give her a minute. "Is that why your girlfriend slapped you in the face and walked off?" Once again I laugh. I can't tell you the last time a woman's humor made me laugh. This girl is pretty amusing.

"She knew I found something more interesting," I say, as I twiddle a strand of her hair between my fingers.

"Is that so?" I expected her to say something clever, but it seems I have stunned her a bit.

"Though, I have thoroughly enjoyed this back-and-forth with you. How about you give me your number so when you're ready, I can show you just how well I can cure that ache between your legs that's happening as we speak." I'm not sure if she will, but I'm surprised at how much I hope she does.

"Just to prove you wrong, how about you give me your number and if I decide I feel like giving that a try, I'll reach out to you." That's better than nothing I guess.

"Do you have a pen?" She looks at me as if she is annoyed, but pulls out a pen from her tiny purse that lays across her body. I follow the strap up over her hips and up to her chest. Her tits are spilling over her royal blue dress, and fuck they look good. I would ever let my girl out of the house looking like that. I'd take her over my knee if she ever did.

"If I wanted to be ogled, I'd go back inside," she says as she pops her hip out and places her hand on her hip once again. "If you didn't want me looking at your big tits, you wouldn't wear a dress like that," I say as I grab the pen out of her hand.

I think that last comment finally shut her up, because when I grab her arm and pull it closer, she doesn't protest. She simply watches me. Taking the pen cap into my mouth, I bite down and release the pen. Once I have written my phone number, large, on her arm, I lean down and blow on her arm. I see goosebumps cover her skin, only it's not chilly out.

She clears her throat and pulls her arm away from mine. Never taking her eyes off of me, she says, "I doubt I'll use this, but it was nice meeting you. Even if I saw more than I intended to." She winks at me and heads back into the bar. My instinct is to go after her, but I've already gotten my dick wet for the night. It's best not to press my luck. Especially since I come here often.

Not bothering to go back inside, I walk down the alley towards my truck. It's a Ford F-150 Lightning Platinum. It's the top of the line with every added feature you could think of. Even my cup holders have warmers.

I quickly drive home to my secluded house on Mercer Island. There are a few homes on the island, but overall it's a very quiet place. Which is exactly what I like.

After being surrounded by several people all day, I just want to be at peace at night.

It's just after midnight when I get home. Luckily for me, it didn't take long to find a willing participant to satisfy my needs.

Once I get inside, I take my shoes off and take a seat on my couch. I look over my dark house. To the outside world, my home looks plastic, sterile, and cold. To me it's a blank canvas for when I find my one.

I've lived here for 3 years, and I've never brought another woman here. No woman needs to be here with me. Why would I let her in if she isn't going to stay?

The floor to ceiling windows let in the sunlight from the moon that's illuminating the night. The water reflects the light making it bounce back at the house. It really is something to revile in.

I decide it's best to sleep. I have work in the morning which requires a lot of attention. It's not my favorite career, but I'm damn good at it. Once my head hits my silk sheets, I'm lost in my thoughts. As always it's of the brown haired woman with no clear image, my one.

Chapter 2 Conrad

It's been 6 days since I've seen the sexy brown haired woman from the bar alley. I've been pretty busy lately so I haven't given much thought to her, but today I can't stop thinking about her. It's probably because I'm reaching my limit on days between pussy, and I bet she has a sweet one.

Maybe I'll go see if she is at the bar tonight.

As soon as I turn off my computer at work, my watch shows 8 pm. I quickly grab my belongings and hop in my truck.

It takes about an hour to get to the bar in this Seattle traffic. Once I arrive, I park and head inside. Hoping to find the sexy brown haired girl right away, I do a lap around the large bar.

To my disappointment, I don't see her. My stomach rumbles signaling I need sustenance if I plan to fuck someone tonight. And I do plan to.

I pick a small table in the corner of the bar and order a steak and salad. The waitress that takes my order is a decently cute blonde. She has thick legs that hold her well shaped ass.

She will do.

When she brings me my meal, I devour it and head over to the bar where she is filling some shot glasses. Once she hands them off, I walk up next to her. She knows who I am. She's worked here for a good 3 months. She's seen me pick up at least 6 different women. She knows what I want.

Placing my hand just about her ass, I play with the hem of her waistband. "Want to show me the back room? I promise, it will be well worth it." She looks up at me and pauses. She's thinking about my request. She's more shy than the other girls. Bold and cocky are surprisingly easier targets.

"Tell me you're not clenching your thighs together imagining my hand between them as I play with your wet pussy," I whisper into her ear as I drop my hand to cup her ass. She doesn't pull away which is a good sign. Dipping my hand down a little lower, I can feel the heat between her legs confirming her desire.

I hear a soft moan come from her lips, it encourages me to continue. Stroking her pussy from behind, I whisper, "Take me back or I'll have to stop." Her eyes land on mine. She is pleading with me not to stop.

She turns on her heels, grabs my wrist, and leads me to a back pantry. I lock the door behind us and immediately give her what she wants. I can tell she needs a little more convincing to drop her panties for me, so I kiss her and play with her clit until she is revving with need. I make sure not to let her get off just yet. "Please," she begs me to let her come.

"Turn around," I say in an angry voice as I make my usual moves. I always turn the women around and fuck them from behind. Even if we are in her bed. She is going to get on her hands and knees for me.

Not wasting any time, I pull a condom on and fuck her until I'm no longer thinking about my one. It's frustrating as hell to only think of one woman, and you don't even know who that woman is.

I make sure the waitress has a mind blowing orgasm because she might need to be a repeat customer, and I want her satisfied, wanting more. After I blow my load into the condom, I give the waitress a nice smile. "I hope to make you see stars again real soon," I tell her, and then I head home for the night without looking back at her.

Chapter 3 Conrad

I've never spent minutes, let alone hours wondering about a woman. Why the fuck has she not reached out yet? It's been 9 days since I saw her, and I'm done waiting.

"Francesca, get Zeak on the phone," I yell into my intercom. "Yes, Mr. Conrad," my assistant cries back.

A few minutes go by and I'm connected with Zeak. "What can I do for you today? I hope it's legal this time," Zeak, my tech guy, says into the phone. He does all kinds of things for me. Most of them are legal. Several of them are in the gray area.

"I want you to look at Bar Xan over by my place. I want you to hack into the security camera in the alleyway out back 9 nights ago. I had an encounter with a brown haired woman. I want her address by the end of the day," I bark out at him.

"You got it boss." He hangs up immediately. This shouldn't be too hard for him. I'm not sure why I haven't done this sooner?

It only takes Zeak 3 hours to send me her address. I decide to end my work day a little early. I'm itching to see her again.

Once I pull up to her house, I sit and wait. It's a decent apartment complex in a good part of town. I wouldn't love for my girl to live here, but I wouldn't overly worry about her safety.

Looking at my watch I see it's just past 7. I've been here for over an hour. I'm a very impatient man, but when it's for something I want, I'll be as patient as I need to be. A small red Chevy Cruze pulls into the apartment complex. The plates match what Zeak gave me.

"There you are my jester," I say out loud. I've been calling her that since it suits her. She's cute and funny like a jester.

I watch her as she gets out of her car and walks up to her second floor apartment. She's dressed in light blue scrubs and her hair is pulled back. She must be a nurse.

After another hour of waiting, she finally emerges from the apartment. Only this time she is dressed in a dark purple crop top and a jean skirt that comes just past her ass. She pairs the outfit with some brown cowboy boots.

Where the hell is this girl going dressed like that? Again, there is no way I'd allow my girl to dress like that. Unless it was for my eyes only.

The brown beauty makes her way back into her car. I follow closely behind her because I doubt she will notice I'm following her. She doesn't seem too observant.

By the time we reach her destination just before 9. It's a hole in the wall Mexican restaurant. My stomach rumbles reminding me I haven't had dinner yet.

Brown beauty bounces to the restaurant and is met with two other women in the same kind of outfit.

They must be single because there is no fucking way a sane man would let his woman go out dressed like that. Maybe I'm not as sane as the next person, but I know what's best.

I watch her with grave interest. She is intriguing. Maybe I can make her my one. Even if she doesn't fit everything I'm wanting, I'll make her fit it.

I watch her eat and drink at the bar. I'm tucked in the corner hoping she doesn't notice me. The place is small, but it's easy to watch her.

She licks her fingers after she finishes her taco. My dick stirs at the image. I can't help but think of her on her knees licking me after I come on her face. Dammit, why can't she have hazel eyes.

Once her and her friends are finished with their food and drinks, they grab their purses and quickly leave the restaurant. Did they not pay? What the fuck?

Thoroughly disappointed, I quickly drop some cash on my table and walk over to the bar to do the same for them. How do they expect a small establishment to survive?

As soon as I drop a couple hundred dollars, I walk fast to catch up to them. Instead of getting back into the car, she walks past it until we arrive at a bar. Great. A country bar. Why are we here? I'm going to be so out of place in my suit and tie.

Once the girls walk inside, I strip off the tie and shove it into my pocket. Unbuttoning the top two buttons, I roll my sleeves up to my elbows. That's a little better, but there's no way in hell I will ever fit in here.

As soon as I step foot into the establishment, all female eyes are on me.

Fuck. That didn't take long.

I head over towards the bar and order a drink. It's my best attempt at blending in. Though I thoroughly stick out as usual.

My eyes watch brown beauty as she dances her cute two-step. Her ass shows with every turn. Though I'm enjoying watching her, I'm getting bored waiting. I usually don't watch women this long, but she has my interest.

It's close to 11 o'clock, and I'm growing restless. I've been watching these three for 2 hours now. I've seen them drown themselves in booze, dance with each other, and now I'm watching them talk to two ass hats.

I'm watching the one that's talking to brown beauty. He's about her height and just placed his arm around her waist. He leans over and whispers in her ear as she giggles. I know if I walked over there, I'd have all three of them eating out of the palm of my hand. Images of having all three of them in bed with me makes my dick twitch.

Now there's an idea.

I can't say I love the fact that this guy has his hands all over her, but it doesn't bother me as much as I thought it would. She's not my one. It will take some work to get her there, If I even can.

I'm all set to go when I see the little bitch slip something into brown beauty's drink.

Are you fucking kidding me? He just drugged her? This guy doesn't deserve to live. Let alone be standing in the same place as me.

Before she can take a drink I make it look as if I accidentally bump into her. I make sure the glass not only spills but drops to the floor. I'd like to shove some broken glass into his throat.

I didn't want to make my presence known, but I can't allow an innocent woman to be drugged, unless I'm the one to do it of course. I'd never take advantage of a woman like that, but sometimes you just need them to listen to you.

I bump into the guy and steal his wallet as I do. He hits brown beauty pretty hard, and her glass drops to the floor. It shatters into several pieces. One is pretty large. It slides over to the bar. Quickly bending over to pocket it before anyone can see it, I'll be using that later.

Another great idea.

"Dude watch it," the prick says to me, but as soon as he sees my size, he puts his hands up in surrender. He moves to the other side allowing brown beauty to lock eyes on me. I raise my eyebrows and pretend to be surprised to see her.

"You didn't have to tackle me to talk to me," she says with a smirk. This girl and her jokes. Someone needs to quiet her mouth up.

"I just couldn't resist," I whisper into her ear. I look up and see the rapist watching us. I'm daring him to try to interrupt us. I'd break his arm before he could even walk over here.

Brown beauty loses interest in the guy as soon as she sees me. I knew she would. Without saying a word I escort her away from the glass and over to the bar. She looks back at her friends as they give her an encouraging wink.

That wasn't difficult at all.

I buy her another drink and slide it over to her. She takes the drink and downs half of it.

She's nervous.

With my hand still on her back I lean into her and whisper, "You really should be more careful beauty. I could have drugged you so easily. Thankfully, I like my women at least halfway awake when I make their toes curl." She clenches her glass harder. Without making eye contact, she leans up against me and whispers back, "Do you like them willing or resistant?"

I think about her question for a moment. Reaching down, I grab the top of her ass and pull her closer to me. Thankfully, it's loud in here so I have to get closer to her. "Both work for me, but I prefer them to beg. Maybe even crawl to me with their mouth wide open."

"I have one question for you," she says as she plays with one of the buttons on my button up dress shirt.

"What's that, Beauty?"

"Is something in your pocket? Or are you just happy to see me?" She says as she leans into me. She's already drunk.

I can't help but chuckle. "I am happy to see you, but It's my tie. I came here right after work."

"That explains the attire," she says as she looks me up and down. I can tell she is enjoying the view.

I nod as she watches me. "Trust me, if I was fully hard, you'd see it from across the room." This time I graze my lips against her cheek. She bites her lip. I can tell she is trying to hide just how turned on she really is. "How about we head back to your place. I'd love to show you what I can do with this tie."

"I'm not showing you where I live, but you can walk me to my car."

Fucking in the car it is.

I keep my right hand on her back as I extend my left arm, gesturing for her to lead the way. I'll walk her to her car, but she isn't driving home. We both know why she wants me to walk her to her car.

She tells her friends and we start walking towards her car. Shit, I forgot how small her car was. Idk how I'm going to fit in there? I really don't want her in my truck.

"Is there something wrong?" She asks as she digs her keys out. It's pitch black with a small streetlight. I could probably screw her against the car and no one would even see us.

"Just imagining you up against the car screaming my name," I say as I trap her body with mine. As soon as she steps back, she falls off the curb, but I catch her before she falls.

"Unlock the door," I say. It's not a question. I've waited all night for her. I've never waited this long for any woman. Maybe I can make her my one. We will have to see how she feels first.

Brown Beauty unlocks the door at my command.
Listens well. Check.

I pull the back door open, but notice how messy her car is.

I guess we won't be laying down.

With the door blocking part of the view, I stand on the other side to give us some privacy.

That will have to do.

Grabbing her chin, I kiss her lips before she can change her mind. I've been wanting to do this for a while now. They are soft, but something is missing. I'm not exactly sure what it is, so I continue.

She kisses me back with need, so I don't wait anymore. I pull her skirt up, tug her panties to the side, and shove my middle finger into her. I'm rewarded with a delicious moan that I greedily swallow with my mouth.

So wet for me. Maybe she could be my one?

Without removing my finger from her pussy, I unbutton my pants with my left hand, careful not to drop the broken glass that's safe inside my pocket. After I get the zipper down, I pull my hard dick out.

Her hands are braced against the car as I insert another finger and push even harder. I don't take my time. I want her to come now, and she does.

Wow. Another thing she's good at.

Sliding my dripping fingers from her, I tear the condom and roll it onto my dick. "Turn around," I demand once again. She does as I say without hesitation. She places her hands on the seat in front of me which gives me great access to her pussy.

I side right in just as I imagined I would. She has been wanting me since the night she saw me fucking the blonde. She got off on watching my dick slam into another woman.

Not something I wanted in my one, but we can work on that.

Just as my fingers were, I'm relentless. I'm not trying to draw out our pleasure. She just got hers, it's my turn now. Just as a car's lights come into the distance I come deep inside her.

"Stay down," I tell her. Once the car passes us, I pull out and toss the condom into the nearby trash can. "I told you your toes would curl."

"I've had better." She shrugs her shoulders as she fixes her skirt. Did she seriously just say that to me? If I didn't have another matter to take care of, I'd bend her over again. Maybe I'd take my time this time.

But my fingers are itching to use this glass shard in my pocket, so I decide to ignore her smart mouth, for now. "Use the number I gave you, Beauty. Next time, I'll take my time and let you come more than twice." I drag my hand down her cheek. I can tell she wants more. I'll gladly give it to her, just not right now.

"We'll see if I still have it." I know she has it written down somewhere. I'm not sure why she is playing hard to get. She knows she's going to use it.

"We both know you still have it." I'm about to walk off when I decide I want to know her name, so I can see how it feels on my tongue. I usually don't care, but I'm experimenting with her. "What's your name, Beauty?"

"It's Rachel. Rachel Evans."

Chapter 4 Conrad

"I'm going to kill you for this," the man on his knees yells out to me, so I tighten my grip on him.

"That was fucking rude. I just wanted to talk. Didn't your mom ever teach you manners?" I antagonize him. This man will soon be dead. I dig in my pocket and pull out the piece of glass that's been hiding in my pocket, waiting for its time to shine.

"Please no, I'm sorry. I'll never do it again." The prick cried out as I pressed the shard of glass to the side of his neck.

"For some reason, I just don't believe you," I say in my calm voice. This guy deserves to die for drugging and raping women. The world will be a better place without him.

"I swear. Here, take them all. I'll even tell you who I got them from." He yells as he continues to plead with me.

Now I'm interested.

"Calm down. Not so loud. My ears are sensitive." I play with his hair just to tease him. "Keep talking," I yell. He actually has some valuable information. "His name is

Roody. He comes to this bar every Friday. I get a handful from him."

Why the fuck would you need so many? Can he not get laid like a normal person? Maybe he gets off on raping women. Bastard. I'd love to watch him cry for his life while I cut his dick off and feed it to the fishes, but I don't have that kind of time, unfortunately.

I'm exposed in this alley, and I really don't feel like getting arrested because of this prick. Ready to go home because it's late and I have work tomorrow, I slice his throat and watch him bleed out.

I pocket some of the pills. You never know when they might come in handy. Taking a deep breath as I stood up, that felt good. The world has one less asshat to worry about.

Let's all shed a tear for this poor lowlife. Pity.

Now the hard part, the clean up. It's the hard part. I love ridding the world of men like this, but I seriously hate disposing of them. But mama always said, "If you want something done right, do it yourself." Bitch, but she is right.

After I wrap him in an old tarp I thankfully found, I shove him into the back of my truck. Tossing several other trash bags on top of him, I'm pleased with how the cleanup went. It looks like I'm headed to the dump, and I am.

As I drive off in peace, I can't help but remember my first kill. You'd think after killing for close to 19 years, I'd start to lose count, but I haven't. I remember every last one of them. I even remember their faces as they begged for their lives.

Some people might say what I do is wrong, but if you really take the time to look at the scum I put in the ground, you'd thank me. They don't deserve to be here.

Who wants a rapist running around? Should I spare that murderer that just killed an innocent woman after robbing her? Do you want your kids running into a pedo? I fucking think not. I'll end each and every one of them.

My first kill was quite humorous actually. I had no clue what I was doing, but I remember it like it was yesterday.

"Conrad, I'm headed out. Make sure you take out the trash," my dad hollers at me. I grab the bag and walk out the front door without complaint. I know it's just better to do as my father asks as soon as he asks. Life is just easier that way.

As I round the corner to the side of the house, I see a man lingering towards the back of the house. I watch him for a moment, wondering why my dog isn't barking at him. "What are you doing back there?" I yell at him. I'm only 18, but I can still hold my own if I need to fight this guy.

He doesn't move at first. Maybe he didn't hear me. As I walk farther towards the back of my house, I hear my dog whimpering. When they come into full view, I see him sitting on my dog with a knife in his hands. Without thinking, I lunged for him. He must have been engrossed in his attempt to kill because as soon as he sees me, it's too late.

My shoulder slams right into his cheek bone. I landed on him hard. The full force of my body immobilizing him. My heart is pounding. I'm not sure if it's from fear that my dog is hurt, or because I'm so furious I want to kill this son of a bitch.

"What did you do to my dog?" I yell at him again, but I quickly realize he is knocked out. With him being dead to the world, I check on Rox. His paws are tied together like the way they tie cows at a rodeo. There is tape around his snout, and he looks out of it. I see no visible signs of him being hurt. There's no blood, but he isn't moving.

Worried, I untie him as fast as possible. The tape is stuck on his fur, so I pull it slowly until it comes free. He blinks and licks his nose, but that's the only movement I get. "What did you give him?" I punch at his chest to wake him up.

Did I really hit him that hard?

I look between Rox and this bastard. I need to get Rox help, but I want answers from this guy. Pausing for what feels like forever, I use the same rope that was once on my dog. I use the same tape to cover his mouth. It's not very sticky, but it will do. This guy has tape, rope, and gave Rox something. He planned this. What monster would do this to a dog?

Not sure what I'm doing, I drag him into our storage shed and tie him to the lawnmower. That should keep him put until I get back. All I know is that he deserves to be punished for this. He doesn't get to get off scot-free. *Where does scot-free even come from? Who is scott? And why is he free?*

I shake my head to bring myself back into focus. Rox. I have to rescue Rox. Scooping him up in my arms, I rush to my truck and lay him in the passenger seat. I drive as fast as I can to the animal hospital.

After an hour, Rox is safe. The jerk had given Rox a paralytic. Thankfully he didn't receive too much or it would have killed him. Though, I'm assuming that's exactly what he had planned to do.

They decide to keep Rox for a few hours just to monitor him. I let them know I'll be back. Then, I drive home like a mad man because that's exactly what I am.

The anger runs through me, ignites once again. I tried to push it back to focus on Rox. Now that I know he is going to be fine, it's time to put all my focus onto this guy.

As soon as I open the shed door, our eyes meet. He has managed to move the tape off of his mouth. "Those screams won't work here. There is no one around for miles," I taunt him. He picked the wrong house to mess with. Most people would have been scared in this situation. I mean, this guy is at least 5 years older than me, but I still outweigh him.

My dad always encouraged me to be fit and know how to handle myself. "You never know when you might need it," he used to tell me. Now, it's just my daily routine. Workout, train, rinse, repeat.

"Let me go, motherfucker or I'll kill you too." Spit flies everywhere. Well that's gross.

His empty threats do nothing to me. It's cute actually. "You think you could kill me? You couldn't even kill my dog," I say as I kneel down. I'm eye level to him. This man that had fury just a moment ago, turns to a scared little girl when I pull out a butcher knife.

"You tried to kill my dog. Why would you do that?" He doesn't answer at first, so I trace the blade along his jaw. The sound it makes sends goosebumps up my skin.

"Because I'm like you man. I like it." Like me? What does that mean? Like me? I'm nothing like this piece of trash. I'd never hurt an innocent animal. Unlike my dog, he deserves to die.

Die? Do I want him to die? The world would be a better place without him, but do I want to kill him? Do I want to be the one to take his last breath?

Yes. I do.

I would be the one to allow him one final breath. I could decide how many more he got. I'd be in charge. I'd be doing the world a kindness to kill this guy.

The thought of sliding my blade into him thrills me. An energy runs through me like I've never felt before. My blade dips into his skin and draws out a single drop of blood.

It's beautiful. The way it runs down his throat to escape my knife. It's as if even the blood knows others will soon follow.

I press in a little harder. The more drops that spill the higher my pulse goes. I can hear his screams in the background, but it's barely audible due to the pounding in my ears.

"I'm sorry. I'll never do it again. Please stop." I can hear him cry. Then, I see the tears run down his face. They glisten on his skin like glass. I can't control myself as I reach out and touch the tears and mix them with his blood.

Beautiful

I'm in a trance. That's the only way I describe what happens next. My knife moves from his jaw down to his *throat, and I slowly push in. The amount of force I exert is equivalent to me pushing on a pen to write on paper.*

I don't force it. I let it glide into his skin. It must be agonizing. Even a sharp blow with a knife would be better than this slow entry, but I can't help it. The way the knife nicks away at each cell, is like art and I, its creator.

Before I know it, the knife is to the base. When my eyes meet his, I see the fear. This is the same fear my dog must have felt. It makes me withdraw the knife swiftly. Again, I'm not sure if it's out of fear, but as I watch the blood pour from his neck, my reality sets in.

Do I regret killing him? No, I don't, but maybe I should have prepared a little more. There is a huge mess, and I only have a couple of hours to dispose of the body and make it look as if I didn't just kill someone.

Thankfully the floor of the shed is just gas. It would have been impossible to clean that up if not. Fumbling over the body, I go to grab a tarp. Just as my foot steps on a rake, it whacks me in the face. "Shit," I can't help but yell.

That hurt. Smooth move. That's going to leave a mark.

After wrapping the body in the tarp, I slowly drag it out to the field behind the house. I go as far as I can, just when my muscles can't pull him anymore.

Good thing he wasn't a fat ass or I'd be here all day.

Running to the house, I grab a shovel and some gloves. Hmmmm, I probably should have put this on first.

Hope nobody finds him. Or I'll be toast.

After thirty minutes of digging, I have a significantly deep hole. He will fit perfectly if I shove him.

It's deep enough that he won't wash away or be easily found.

Once I've covered him up with dirt, I lay down in the grass and welcome the cool rain. It's like a thank you from the heavens. I have rid the earth of a psychopath.

You're welcome.

Damn, my eye was bruised for weeks. I had blisters on my hands, but it was worth every splinter I got. I chuckle at the memory.

Good times.

Chapter 5 Conrad

    Rachel Evans, this girl is about to piss me off. I've been watching her on and off for six days. Six days this girl has gone without texting me. I know she's been itching to. I can tell by the way she cracks her knuckles and rubs her thighs together that she's itching to have me again.

    So stubborn, Beauty.

    As I'm sitting in my car watching her as I do every night through her apartment window, I see her staring at her phone. I'm close enough to see she is on a messaging app, but I'm not close enough to see what it says.

    I feel my phone vibrate deep inside my pocket. A smile speeds across my face as soon as I see the message.

    Rachel: "You miss me yet?"

    Finally! Oh Beauty, no I don't miss you. I've been watching you this whole time.

    I will say I miss the way my dick felt going inside of her, but maybe I shouldn't say that to her just yet. I'll just play with her.

    Conrad: Depends who this is.

    I know damn well who this is. I'm watching her text me. I can see the scowl on her face when she reads my message.

Rachel: That better be some lame ass joke.

She sounds upset. I'm going to have to teach her some manners.

Conrad: I'm sorry, I don't have you saved in my contacts.

I'm just fucking with her. Seeing her stand up and throw her phone onto the couch and immediately go back over to get it has me rolling. She can't help herself.

Rachel: Dick!

Damn, this girl has an attitude problem. Good thing I'm well versed in fixing those.

Conrad: Ahh, so you do think about it.

Conrad: When was the last time you thought about me?

Conrad: When your hand slid down into your panties last night?

Conrad: Did it not satisfy you? Is that why you're texting me now?

She doesn't text me back right away. I'm sure I gave her pause. I'm sure she is thinking about me sliding between her folds.

Rachel: You wish.

Conrad: Of course I do. I'm an honest man. I can admit I want to be deep inside you right now.

Conrad: Before you make up something about not fantasizing about my hands between your legs, just don't. Meet me at Boozers in 1 hour or don't bother. I don't play the hard to get game.

It's risky to be so blunt with her, but it's true. I'm not chasing anyone. I don't care what they can do for me. I don't care how sweet their pussy tastes.

After several moments, I saw her start typing. She hits send and rushes off further into the apartment. My assumption is she is going to get ready.

Rachel: You know, I don't even know your name? You could be some serial killer.

I almost spew out my water as I read her text. If only you knew.

Conrad: Conrad. Now that's enough questions. I'll see you in 1 hour.

Rachel: Fine.

Not exactly the response I was looking for, but at least she is coming. And I'm going to make sure she comes several times tonight.

I've spent a couple of hours a day watching Rachel after work. She has her routine. Work, come home, shower, watch tv, read, go to sleep, repeat. She rarely goes out until her friends convince her to. Lucky for me, she makes it easy to watch her.

I watch as she fidgets with her nails as she walks into the bar. She's nervous. Good. I've never been here, but I watched Rachel come here with her friends yesterday, so she must be comfortable here.

I watch her as she walks up to the bar and scans the room. She's looking for me, wondering if I'm here yet.

Oh I'm here beauty. Little do you know, I have big plans for you.

I did some research on her company. They are being bought out by some large corporations . They are closing their doors, so she will soon be out of a job. I can use that to my advantage.

I'll save you, Beauty. I have a plan. Don't worry.

She pulls out her phone and types on it. Right away, I feel my phone buzz.

Rachel: How long are you going to make me wait?

Damn this girl is feisty. I'm going to have to tame her.

Conrad: How about you turn that ass of yours around.

She whips her body around and sees me right behind her. "You have a mouth on you, I can't wait to use it in other ways," I say as I press up against her side.

She squares her hips and replies, "Oh I'm sure you'd thoroughly enjoy that, but maybe I'm not that kind of girl." She pushes against me trying to create space, but I don't go anywhere. I wrap my arm around her waist and pull her closer.

"Someone needs to teach you some manners. Luckily for you, I'm just the guy." I can see her heart pounding against her low cut dress. Ain't no fucking way my girl would wear this out in public.

Oh Beauty, you have so much to learn.

"Who says you're that guy? Maybe he's that guy," she points to some random guy sitting at the bar. I chuckle at how ridiculous this girl is. "The only thing he is going to teach you is how to fall asleep during sex." I push her up against the bar. A couple of people look over at me, but I ignore them. This doesn't concern anyone else. Only me and this woman that is determined to piss me off.

The guy to my left stands up as if he is going to help this girl I'm about to teach a lesson to. I stare at him as a warning.

Fuck with me and I will end you.

He takes the hint and sits back down. "Someone really needs to teach that mouth of yours some manners." I pull her to the back room without saying another word.

"Where are you taking me?" She calls out as I pull her with me. She has to run to keep up with my fast stride. Her heels slam against the dirty floor and it makes me smile knowing what's about to come.

As soon as I see a closet I open the door and shove her inside. Flicking on the light, I watch her. Without taking my eyes from her, I notice the room is full of canned foods and cleaning supplies.

Not the most romantic spot, but it will do for teaching this girl a lesson. "Where are we back here, Conrad?" I see her pulse rise at the uncertainty. Her legs slap together as I look her up and down with an evil grin. She has a pretty decent figure. She's taller than what I picture my one being, but definitely something I can work with.

"Get on your knees, Beauty."

Chapter 6 Rachel

"Closing?" I yell into the phone. Seriously? My company is closing? What am I going to do now? How am I going to pay my bills?

I can't help but cry into my pillow. I feel like a little girl, but I loved my job. It paid well and was really close to my apartment. I'll never find something that good. Most companies don't pay their people well unless they have an RN license, and I don't have time for that.

My mind goes to Conrad. He asked me to have lunch with him today, but I had said no because I had to work. I sniffle as I wipe my tears.

Apparently I'm free now.

That's definitely not how I wanted to see Conrad. It would be nice to be around him, but I'm not much in the mood for anything other than crying.

Things have been going surprisingly well with him. He's a bit on the doom and gloom side. He always has a scowl on his face and I'm not so sure he is a nice person, but fuck me if he isn't the sexiest man I've ever seen.

We've been seeing each other on and off for a couple of weeks now. He's never asked me to lunch before. Are we already at the "day date" stage of dating? I can't help but smile at the thought. At least I have him. I pull out my phone and send him a text.

Rachel: Welp, looks like I am free today. I just got canned. My company is shutting down. What the hell am I going to do?

It's nine in the morning, so I don't expect him to reply for a while. Tossing my phone onto the bed, I pick out my outfit and shower. I want to be ready for our lunch date when he messages me. I sure hope he can still meet me.

An hour later, I hear my phone ping. I'm on my bed blowing my nose into a wadded up kleenex. I've been crying this whole time just thinking about my job.

My heart flutters when I see it's Conrad. I don't know what it is about this guy. I can't put my finger on it, but he is…different. I haven't decided if it's in a good way or not. But the man can screw like his life depends on it. I'm still shaking from the last orgasm he gave me and it's been several days.

Conrad: We will find you something. I'll be over in 20 minutes.

He is coming here? I am a mess. I thought I'd have time to calm down and get pretty before I met him.

Rachel: Ok.

I send the text and rush around to get ready. I don't want him seeing me like this.

Conrad: Don't just say OK.

I don't see his message until just before I hear him knocking on my door.

Crap. That was fast.

I dab at my eyes to make sure my makeup isn't smeared. I'm dressed in jeans and a cute t-shirt. It's nothing fancy. I just wasn't in the mood to dress up.

As soon as I open the door, he grabs my phone.

"Oh so you did get my message," he says as he walks inside. A ball of nerves form inside my stomach. He looks mouthwatering. He's in a dark gray fitted suit. I can see all of his muscles begging to come out.

As he walks further into my apartment. he peels off his jacket.

Oh the gods heard my prayers.

Even though I'm emotionally drained, my pussy mustn't have gotten the memo. Because it's starting to leak.

He rolls his sleeves up as if he is about to build furniture in a suit. He can do whatever he wants as long as I can watch him undress. Does he want to have sex? Before I opened the door, I would have said no. But seeing him now, my body is screaming yes.

Instead of taking off more clothes, he sits on my couch and waves me over. "Come here."

I immediately obey, because I want whatever he is about to give me. Maybe it will make me feel better. He pulls me onto his lap and holds me. He doesn't make a move or try anything sexual. He just holds me.

"We will find you a job. I know it's scary right now, but it will all work out." His words are sweet. This is a new side of Conrad.

I can't help but let silent tears fall. He holds me for what feels like days, but in reality it's probably only an hour.

Being this close to him relaxes me like I never thought it would . Usually when I'm around him, I want sex. But having him show me his sweet side, it has me wanting more with him.

He touches the side of my check and kisses it. My tears have long stopped thanks to him. I'm starting to fall for this man, it's clear. I think it's safe to say that once I let go, I'll be falling so hard I'm going to crash and burn.

Conrad stayed for about two hours. Then, he had to go back to work. I miss him already.

I hear my phone buzz as it sits on the TV stand.

Conrad: Be at Marcelo's in one hour.

I do a happy dance because I'm shameless in my excitement. Not only do I get to see the smoldering hot Conrad again, but I get to eat at Marcelo's. It's the finest Italian restaurant we have. Of course he would get us in there.

I still don't know much about him, but I know he has his own financial firm. I can tell he has money coming out of his ears. He doesn't talk about much else though.

Rachel: You got it dude.

I wait for his text before I finish getting ready.

Conrad: Don't ever fucking call me dude again.

Jeez. I was just trying to be funny. Note to self, Conrad doesn't like to be called "dude", but I can't help myself. He gets mad so easily.

Rachel: You got it boss.

Conrad: Boss? I like the sound of that. Maybe I should be your boss.

Boss? How would he be my boss? I have a LPN license. I don't know the first thing about finance, nor do I want to.

Rachel: Like role play? Or for real?

I wait for his reply, but nothing comes. Ugh. Why is he not texting me back? It's been 30 minutes and nothing. He is doing this on purpose just to get to me. So why am I letting him?

Rushing to get ready, because I took way too long staring at my phone in hopes it would force a response somehow. It didn't, unfortunately.

Pulling up to the restaurant right at 6 pm, I spot a beautiful black F150. Conrad is already here. Damn if that truck isn't the sexiest truck. It's perfect for him. I'd love to try that bed out for sure.

I park right next to him, and I can't help the ball of nerves forming in my stomach. "Ms. Evans, so nice to see you," he says as he sticks out his hand. Is he seriously wanting to shake my hand? What the hell?

I slide my hand into his because why not? I love to feel his strong hands on me anywhere. "Why are we shaking hands?" I asked with a confused look on my face.

"This is now a business meeting. Please, come this way." He sticks out his hand to lead me inside the restaurant.

What is going on?

Once we find our seats, he pulls out my chair for me. Wow. I've never had a guy do that for me. "Please take a seat." I cautiously take my seat, never taking my eyes off of him. His demeanor is different. Does he really want this to be a business meeting? If so, why?

I don't speak. I simply watch him because that's the only thing I can do. It's as if my body doesn't have any other choice but to watch him. He is absolutely gorgeous and my eyes enjoy every moment. "You're staring Ms. Evans. Is there something on your mind?" He asks as he peers over his menu.

"No, just waiting for the business part of our lunch," I tease as I put up my menu and pretend to scan it. I have no clue what I'm doing. It's as if I've forgotten how to read. I'm that girl in the middle of English class when the teacher calls on her to read and she hasn't been following along.

I'm lost and it's all because of him.

"Should we share some spaghetti Lady and the Tramp style? You can have my meat ball," he jokes. I think that might be the first time I've seen him show all of his teeth when he smiles.

Damn, I'd say he should do that more often, but I'm not sure my heart could take it. "Does that make you the tramp?" I tease back.

That smile of his is gone now, leaving me longing for it. "Oh I'd never be a beggar, but I do search for what I want quite often," he replies without taking his eyes off the menu.

Why would he think I thought he'd beg? And what is he searching for? He must see my confusion because he continues speaking. "'Tramp' is another word for beggar or searcher. I don't beg, but I quite often search for what I want. Which is why we are here."

50

"How would you feel about me begging?" His eyes turn mischievous. "You can beg all you want. I'd enjoy that immensely, but in the end I'll give you what you deserve and nothing more."

His words are cold. I'm not sure if I like it or not. Who am I kidding? Anything he does I like.

"I thought this was a business meeting?" I question as I raise my eyebrows at him. "That doesn't seem very professional." I use air quotes as I tilt my head.

"You're right. Let's get to business," he says just as the waiter comes and takes our order. I decided against the spaghetti although sharing anything with him is tempting. I get my favorite, manicotti with à la Panna sauce. Conrad orders lobster ravioli. It sounds delicious.

Maybe he will share it with me.

We talk about my job and what I've done for the past eight years since getting my license. I tell him how I've been with the same company. I was extremely loyal to them and them to me. Which is a huge reason it breaks my heart they had to close down.

Conrad reassured me that it's for the best, but I can't help but think how much I'm going to miss it there. But maybe he's right, maybe a fresh start is exactly what I need. I'm trying to convince myself. Now, I just have to figure out what that new start looks like.

"I don't talk about my past much, but I have a mother that is in need of long-term care. I recently had to let go of my employee. She wasn't what I wanted anymore. Is that something you would be interested in?"

Is he offering me a job? Not only am I being offered a position to work for the man I'm dating, but now I have to wrap my mind around the fact that this cold man has a poor mother that's in need of long-term care.

Why hasn't he mentioned her before?

"Are you offering me a job?" I'm still confused as to how this would work? Can I still date him? Because I don't want to give him up. He is too good to lose. Sure, I've only been dating him a short time, but he's got me hooked.

Watching him as he leans back in his chair and crosses his arms, I see the tension in his shoulders. I want nothing more than to rub them for him. I want to ease him of any negativity or stress he might have.

"I am," he answers. No other details. Whatever it is, yes. I want it as long as I can still date him. "What's your concern?" He asks, noticing my unsure look.

"If I work for you, can I still date you?" I ask him point blank because there is no point in beating around the bush. I'd choose him over a job in a second.

"I don't see why that would be a problem, do you?" I simply shake my head. No problem here whatsoever.

"Then it's settled. You will start tomorrow." I can't help but smile as the waiter brings over our food. We eat in silence as we steal glances from each other.

I'm not sure how this job is going to be, but at least I have Conrad to depend on.

Chapter 7 Conrad

I didn't fuck her today. I didn't have time after our lunch date. My dick is still cursing at me, but it will live. I still have to get back to the office and grab my things. I have a sweet old lady waiting in a mansion for me. The memory of finding Barbara floods me.

This spot is perfect. It's secluded, and the owner is a little old lady that used to be a defense attorney. No, she never physically hurt anyone, but she used to get rapists, pedophiles, and murders off. That just doesn't sit well with me. I don't plan on killing her, but using her for what I need will be sufficient.

She lives alone. Husband is dead. Her daughter just died. She has no other living relatives. She doesn't have any close friends. Apparently her job made her unlikable, imagine that. She's the perfect mark. So here I am, ready to take over her life as if it were mine.

I watch as she wanders around her home without a care in the world. Little does she know, she is my next target.

Sneaking in is easy. I've watched her for several days. I know her routine. It's just about time for her to have her cup of tea and take a bath. Ain't no fucking way I'm drugging this lady while she is naked. I'm a lover of all things female, but I draw the line somewhere.

Pulling out my lock pick, I easily unlock the side door. It slides open as my expert hands handle it. Just like a woman's body. You touch it the right way, and it will open wide for you.

Pleased with myself, I quietly entered the house. It's darker than it usually is, so I use that to my advantage. I quickly spot her in the kitchen warming up her usual tea. Only the under cabinet lights are on which allows me to sneak in behind her.

I stand there and watch her. My pulse races from the anticipation. I feel a slight sweat growing on the back of my neck. I'm not nervous. This is just new. I've done similar things many times, but I've never targeted an older woman. I'm almost excited.

As soon as she turns to walk out of the kitchen, I grab her tea and pour the crushed up pills into it. I watch as they dissolve quickly in the hot water. I decided to use one of the date rape drugs from the scum at the bar. I have lots of medicine I could choose from, but I was curious how well this would work.

I slide back into the shadows as she returns. Her silk robe drags on the ground as she walks. She's a tiny old woman. Hopefully that drug won't be too much for her.

It's as if she can sense me. She turns around and whispers, "Hello. Is someone there?" I've never understood why people do that? Why would you make it easier for your intruder to find you by speaking?

She clutches her tea as if it's going to save her. Little does she know, that's exactly what will be her demise.

She takes a step closer to me. If she keeps walking, she will find me. She will discover my position, and so will have to use force. Shit. I really don't want to subdue this woman. Though she deserves it, I don't want to break her brittle bones.

Just as she is about to reach the shadows I hide in, she stops. "Is that you Margaret? I swear this house is haunted." She turns and walks out of the kitchen.

Who the fuck is Margeret? It's probably someone haunting her.

Ten minutes later I emerge from my shadow. I haven't heard her make any noise in a while. Venturing out into the large living room, I spot her. She is out on her recliner. Spilling the tea on her way down, she barely makes it to the recliner.

I guess those drugs worked fast on the old woman.

I work as fast as possible. Getting her settled into the bed was easy. Hauling in all the supplies I need to keep this broad asleep for the time being was the difficult part.

Thankfully Barbara is a small woman. If she had been large, my back would be killing me by now. I have had to lift her and move her several times. Once she is in the bed, I start setting everything up for Rachel tomorrow.

By the time I'm finished it's well into the morning. I guess I'll only be getting two hours of sleep today. It's worth it. Now I can start making Rachel my one.

I've settled into the mansion nicely. It's been a few days since I broke in and took over. I'm tired as balls from all the work this has taken, so I took the day off of work. Plus, I can rest later. I'd say I'm pleased with how everything went. Barbara is looking good on the medication. As long as she is given her dosage at the appropriate time, everything should be fine. Rachel will be here any minute. She better be on time.

I'll keep Barbara asleep and Rachel close while I mold her into what I want. She's not perfect, but I'm tired of waiting. I'll force her to be perfect.

"Hello," I hear the soft whisper coming from the side door. "Come in," I invite her in as I meet her in the kitchen.

"You seriously live here? Holy hell. I knew you had money but fuck me," Rachel bellows as she walks around without permission. She really needs to be taught some manners.

Not in the mood for pleasantries, I go through everything with her. I show her Barbara's room and the medication she needs. I decided to keep it locked up to look more professional.

I inform Rachel of her duties I expect her to fulfill. She makes some joke about me using the word duties. You'd think this woman was 15 and not almost 30.

"Do you have any questions for me?" I try to stay in professional mode.

"What do I do during my free time?" She tilts her head to the side and runs her hand down the side of her neck. She's trying to tempt me. While my dick is jumping at the chance to get wet, I don't have the energy to fuck her the way I'd like to.

"When you're done with your shift, you can come ride my dick," I say as if I told her to go grab a drink of water. It's no big deal.

I wait for her to respond, but she doesn't. She is shifting her weight back and forward on either leg. She's nervous. That's funny. She's come on my dick a handful of times already. I'm not sure why she is still nervous about it.

"If I feel like it after such a long day," she finally snaps back. This girl. She likes to play like she isn't interested, but by the way her legs rub together, she is begging to get off by my touch.

"You will. I'll meet you in the kitchen at 5. We will have dinner and then dessert." I give her a serious look because we both know that she is going to be my dessert. I lick my lips at the thought, turn, and walk away.

It's been about two weeks since Rachel started. It's been a while since I've seen Rachel around the house, so I go and check in on her. She seems to be doing just fine with Barbara. I've spent the better part of the week getting my new office arranged without her noticing. This is my home for the foreseeable future. I might as well play the part.

I had to keep my door closed and locked because she kept coming to find me. I can tell she is going to be a needy one. I'll have to fix that too.

I stick to my routine. Work, sleep, workout, fuck, but I've stopped actively searching for my one. I'm doing my best to make Rachel her. She still has so much to learn and change. I'm still not certain it will work.

After getting my daily workout in and sending some emails, it's close to 4 o'clock. My dick stirs at the thought sinking into her link folds. It's been too long since my dick has been inside of her. I've been too busy getting everything settled, so it's excited at the thought.

Grabbing my phone, I order Chinese food for us. Most places won't deliver all the way out here, but if you throw enough money at anyone they will do what you want.

Showering longer than I usually do, I rest on the bench in my new master shower. It has heated stones. I have money, but this place screams cash. Everything is luxurious. Everything is above and beyond someone's needs.

I should probably pull out money from Barbara's account just in case this thing goes sideways and I need to escape. It would probably be suspicious if the owner of a financial firm took out thousands of dollars.

As I sit, I allow the hot water to run down my body. My back is pressed firmly against the shower wall. The cold wall mixed with the hot water is a pleasurable marriage.

My mind drifts off to her head between my legs. It's not Rachel. It's her. She appears on the floor. I can't see her whole face because the stream is filling the shower, but I can feel her hands snake up my legs and land on my hardening dick.

It feels so real, I almost open my eyes to make sure Rachel didn't crawl into the shower with me. I wouldn't put it past her.

No, it's not Rachel. It's someone else. She looks similar to Rachel, but she has hazel eyes. She has the eyes of my one. I hold my eyes closed as tightly as I can. I don't want the vision to leave. I want to hold onto her as long as possible.

I'm tempted to start fucking my hand, but I don't want to risk any movement. I'm terrified to lose this image. The image of my one on her knees, for me. She looks up at me with those brown, green eyes, and I almost come right there.

Why can't you be real? Why can't I find you?

Just as my one is about to wrap her lips around my needy dick, I hear my name being called, and the visual is gone. No longer am I seeing her on her knees.

"Fuck," I let out a growl. I'm pissed. I'm fucking pissed. The shower steam is no longer what fills the room. It's the fire coming from me.

Why did this girl ruin my daydream?

"Are you alright, Conrad?" Rachel questions as she walks into the bathroom.

No I'm not fucking alright. I'm seething. I don't want to take my anger out on her, but I do. Jumping out of the shower, I grab a handful of her hair. Pulling her closer, I smash her tits against me so hard I hear her whimper.

Her lips tilt towards mine. She is begging to be kissed, so I kiss her as hard as I can. It's as if I'm trying to physically mold her into the girl in the shower.

She places her hands on my chest and shoves me back. "What's going on?" She pulls back and looks at me with concern. I seriously don't want her talking. It's pulling me from the image I'm trying to hold onto.

I grab the base of her shirt and pull it over her head as fast as humanly possible without ripping her head off with it. I like blood, but not from the woman I'm about to fuck.

She grabs my dick and starts pumping it. She's eager, and so am I. It's been too long. Little does she know, I'm mentally screwing the woman from the shower. I think I'll keep that part to myself for now.

"You're so hard. You must have been thinking about me in the shower, huh? I love how hard you get for me," she moans.

I just want to tell her to shut up. Stop talking. Instead, I rip off her bra and shove it into her mouth. "Take that out and I'll stop giving you what you want. Do you understand?" I question her. She simply nods her head.

She's usually a feisty one, but going several days without my dick has her on edge too. I'll have to remember that. She's easier to control when she's deprived and desperate .

Spinning her around as if we are dancing, I slam her against the countertop. When I look into the mirror, I see shock in her brown eyes. Although the fear is beautiful, I don't want to see her eyes right now. I want to see my ones eyes.

I shove her head down further so she is no longer visible in the mirror. With one swift motion, her leggings and panties are on the ground. Pushing her feet apart as wide as I can with her pants still around her ankles, I slide my hand around to feel her swollen nub.

Just as I expected, she grinds against my hand. Desperate for the release she knows I will give her.

She sticks her ass out, begging me to give her the attention she truly desires. My dick. I smack her ass as I grind my pelvis against her, letting her know it's time. I'm tired of waiting. Getting ready Beauty.

With one swift motion, I go from teasing her to balls deep. "Ahh," she tries to scream, but her cries are muffled from her own bra that's shoved into her mouth. I like her like this, quiet and needy.

I'm taking my anger out on her with my dick. Pounding harder and harder into her, I lose myself in the daydream. Those eyes are watching me through the steam. They are drawing me in. They want me to come closer. They want me to find her.

I can feel my hips burning from the force I'm applying as I continue slamming into her. I'm starting to tighten. I'm not sure I want to find my release just yet. I know as soon as I do, the image of the girl in the shower will fade.

I haven't even been focusing on Rachel. I don't know if she is enjoying herself. I don't know if she is in pain or feeling pleasure? I'm not sure I care at the moment. I can make it up to her later if I need to.

My knees start to shake as I angle my dick upwards. I slow down my pace for a moment, enjoying the tightening around me. I'm being squeezed. Her pussy is pulsating. She must have just had an orgasm, but again, I'm not focusing on her right now.

Picking up my pace once again, I grab onto her shoulder and pull her back so she is meeting my thrusts. "Fuck, yes." I'm not going to last much longer. Especially, with those hazel eyes staring up at me from the shower floor. Picturing her mouth wrapping around my dick and I'm done. I pull out just in time as my load covers her back.

My breathing is erratic. I'm having a hard time catching my breath. Forcing myself to see how Rachel is, she has sunk to the floor. Her leggings are still around her ankles. The look on her face says she enjoyed herself. With her rosy cheeks and heaving chest, I'd say she got off a couple of times at least.

"Well that was wild," she says between pants. I don't answer her. I simply nod in response.

I was right, as soon as I came, the vision of my one disappeared. I'm in a worse mood than before.

Just as I'm about to tell her I need to get back to work, I hear the doorbell. Shit, the food. "Get dressed and come eat," I tell her as I stand up and slide my black joggers on.

"What's with your mood today?" She snaps back at me as she pulls her leggings up. I look back at her.

You seriously don't want to start with me today woman.

Instead of saying this to her, I walk over to her, grab her jaw slightly, and kiss her. It's hard, but not hard enough to hurt her. "Just do what I said."

I'm not in the mood to argue with her. If she continues with her attitude, I might end up beating her ass.

Walking out of the bedroom before she can smart off to me, I grab my wallet. Opening the door, I'm taken aback. Standing in the doorway with my food is a cute little brunette. I can't help but eye her up and down as I check out her nice figure. She's too pretty to be delivering food for a restaurant.

Her eyes are locked onto my bare chest which makes me laugh. I watch her until her eyes finally find mine. Her throat clears, and her cheeks turn red.

How cute.

"Sorry. Um, here you go," she hands me the food. Her hands rub against her jeans. Her palms must be sweaty. She doesn't know what to do next. I can't help but smile at her and find amusement at making her nervous.

"What do I owe you, sweetheart?" I ask her as I lean against the doorframe. Her eyes light up at the pet name.

That was too easy. If I hadn't just gotten off, I'd try my luck with her. "Is that our food?" I jump at the sound of Rachel. I literally forgot she was here.

Wow.

What is wrong with me?

"Um, yeah." I give the cute girl three 20 dollar bills and shut the door before she can say anything else. I don't want Rachel giving me lip. I'd have to correct her behavior, and I'm not in the mood for it.

We sit in silence and eat our Chinese food. I ordered us way too much. Rachel likes to have leftovers when she comes the next day.

See, I'm nice to her.

"That was so good. Thank you for getting this," she kisses my cheek as she throws her plate away.

"I'll put the leftovers in the fridge for you," I tell her as I finish off my plate. I've never liked leftovers, but she is welcome to them. When I was pretty young, we had leftovers all the time. I guess I got tired of it.

"I guess it's time for me to go," she says as she pouts. She's literally sticking her lip out, trying to get me to ask her to stay the night. It's not that I want her to be in my bed, but I have to make sure Barbara is well sedated. Plus, I like my alone time.

"I will see you tomorrow morning. Don't give me that lip. I'll bite it off," I threaten. Her eyes widen because she knows I'm telling the truth. She quickly sucks her lip back in.

That's better.

"I just wish I didn't have to go. Do you want to come over to my place tonight?" Rachel asks as she grinds her tits against me.

She's trying to tempt me again after I blew my load on her. I have no energy left. I have to get some sleep tonight. I have several meetings in the morning. Plus, I don't sleep very well with someone.

"Maybe tomorrow. I need to get some work done tonight. I'll see you in the morning," I say as I usher her out of the door.

"You're not even going to give me a kiss goodnight?" She pouts her bottom lip once again. If I wasn't so annoyed, I'd probably bite that lip of hers for pouting. I just fucked her into oblivion, and she is pouting?

Seriously?

She's starting to annoy me. What was I thinking? How am I supposed to mold her into my one?

Taking a deep breath, I kiss her stuck out lip and smack her ass. I'm not ready to give up on her just yet. Maybe there's still hope for her.

The next two days go by like a blur. I haven't seen Rachel at all today, but I'm fine with that. I needed a break from her. She's starting to get too clingy. She basically camped out in my office yesterday. I finally had to kick her out. I'm not sure how to break her of this?

It's about 9 o'clock at night when I hear my doorbell ring.

Who the fuck could that be?

As soon as I open the door, my jaw drops. It's the cute girl from two nights ago. The one that delivered the food. Why is she here?

"Oh darn, you have a shirt on tonight," she says jokingly.

I can take it off just as fast as I can get your pants off. I want to say, but figure I better not. I have Rachel.

"I do. The other night you caught me just out of the shower. You're lucky I had pants on." I unintentionally flirt with her.

Her eyes go wide. I'm guessing she wished she had. "I wouldn't have complained," she says as she reaches up with her right hand playing with her lower lip. Her left hand goes under her right elbow as she watches me with hungry eyes. She watches me as if I'm her meal tonight.

What the hell is going on?

The balls on this one to come here and act this way. She seemed so timid the other night. Maybe she was just surprised that I was the one that lived here. Sexy shirtless man in a mansion, that only happens in the movies.

"Is that right?" I wait for her response, but she simply nods. Her nails are now between her teeth. She's biting them in a nervous way. It's cute.

Staring at her, I cross my arms and lean against the doorframe. What does she want?

"Can you show me?" She lifts her head towards me. At first I think she wants to come inside, but now I'm not so sure.

"What are you wanting to see?"

A grin comes across her face, "you without a shirt on, of course."

I know I shouldn't, but I can't help myself. I mean, what am I supposed to do? A sexy little thing comes to my door and basically throws herself at me? What's a guy to do?

I grab the back of my tshirt and pull it over my head. Her eyes go to my exposed chest. Instead of saying another word, she takes control. This shocks me because I'm not usually attracted to dominant girls.

Her hands explore my chest, running her fingers up and down my abs. Before I know it, she starts pulling my joggers down.

Fuck.

"You probably shouldn't, I have a-a person." I'm not sure what Rachel is?

"I noticed," she says but it doesn't stop her hand from pulling out my dick.

Shit. What is this girl doing? Am I in a dream? This doesn't happen in real life.

"Wow." She watches my dick harden in her hand. I can't help it. I should stop her, but I don't. I mean, she has my dick in her hand.

She slowly goes to her knees, and pulls me into her mouth.

"Fuck." I'm incapable of stopping her now. My hands dive into her hair as I pull her closer. She gags but doesn't stop.

Her mouth is warm against the cool air. She is sucking me off on the front porch with the door still open. That's it, I must be dreaming.

She doesn't stop sucking and pumping me until she has drained me dry. A loud moan escapes my mouth as I come deep into her mouth.

She stands up, wipes the corners of her mouth, and says, "are you going to invite me in?" I open the door wider, not saying a word. I have zero intention of talking with this girl, but I will be using her.

My mind goes to Rachel. Is this what guilt feels like? I've never had a person before her. We haven't put a label on us, so maybe I'm not doing anything wrong.

I shrug to myself as I shut the door behind us. My dick is still hanging out of my pants. It's already starting to get hard again.

"Now, where were we?"

Chapter 8 Rachel

It's been a weird couple of weeks. Conrad doesn't seem to be acting the same as he was. He has been distant. We don't talk much. As soon as I finish my shift, he drags me to his bed or wherever he wants me, bends me over and fucks me until I see stars.

Don't get me wrong, it's amazing, but I've fallen in love with the man. I want more, and I still know nothing about him. Can you really love someone you don't know?

"I love you," I let slip as we both come down from a mindblowing orgasm. He stiffens as he quickly pulls out of me. I'm not sorry I said it. It's how I feel. He should love me too. We are meant to be together.

I spin around to make sure he heard me. He won't make eye contact with me. He simply kisses me on the cheek and zips up his jeans.

Seriously? He's just going to ignore me?

"Did you hear me?" I know he did.

"I did." That's it. No other explanation.

"So you don't feel the same way? We screw like rabbits. How can you not feel the same?" I feel panic. Tears start to form in my eyes.

"We've only been together for less than two months." He says it so matter of fact like. Like I don't already know that. Like I'm crazy for feeling this way.

"So what. People can fall in love faster than that. Have you ever heard of Love At First Sight?"

"I have heard of it, but it's just something people say. It's not real. People don't fall in love right away." He doesn't even seem bothered by this conversation.

"Wow. That's the stupidest thing I've ever heard, and you're stupid for thinking that way." As soon as I say it, I know I'm wrong.

His eyes darken and he grabs the base of my neck. He doesn't hurt me, but it scares me. "You better watch what you say to me, Rachel. Just because you're upset, doesn't give you the right to act crazy."

Did he just call me crazy? What the fuck. I shove at him as hard as I can. Surprisingly he stumbles back one step. It's not as much as I was hoping for, but I'm surprised he moved at all.

"Don't call me crazy," I yell at him. I've never been this mad at him before. He crossed a line.

"I think it's time for you to go before I take my anger out on you, and it won't be pleasurable like it usually is." He points to the door. I'm on the verge of crying. My blood is boiling. I'm enraged.

"Screw you, Conrad," I yell as I slam the door behind me. I can't believe he just said that to me. This night went very differently than I had imagined. I told him I loved him, and he called me crazy.

How can I work for someone like that? What am I going to do?

I drive home and let the tears fall. The love of my life has just broken my heart. My boss just kicked me out. Does that mean I don't have a job anymore?

Pulling up to my apartment, I dry my eyes with my jacket sleeve. I'd love to say he isn't worth crying over him, but he is. He is the most amazing man. I love him.

Stepping out of my car, the rain slaps my face. At least no one would be able to tell I've been crying if they see me. Not that anyone is around to see.

I feel broken. I need him in my life. I don't know what I'd do if he left me.

The tears fall as I open my apartment door. It feels nice and warm inside. I rub my arms because I realize I'm shaking. I'm not sure if it's from the cold rain or the thought of losing Conrad.

Crawling into bed, I hold my favorite teddy bear as I cry myself to sleep. This can't be the end. Can it?

Chapter 9 Conrad

"What the fuck was that?" I say to myself. I'm still pissed off and it's been an hour since Rachel left.

She loves me?

How can she say that? Maybe I shouldn't have called her crazy, but you can't love someone after two months. It hasn't even been two months. That's crazy.

Feeling the need to get out of the house, I check on Barbara. Once I see she is good, I get in my truck and drive. I'm not sure where I'm driving to, but I drive around Seattle for about an hour before I end up almost back where I started.

I'm just a few miles from the mansion. Spotting a restaurant with outside seating, I pull into the parking lot. I'm a sucker for outside seating that's covered.

The rain has let up, but you can still smell it. I don't love the weather here, but I do love the smell of fresh rain.

As soon as I enter the restaurant, I asked to be seated outside. The hostess leads me outside. "Have a seat wherever you like."

I take a look at the patio. There are at least twenty tables out here. The outline of the patio has a bar table top that looks over the city.

I pick a seat in the far right corner. It makes it easier to watch people. It's not too busy yet, but it will be since it's Friday. I don't like having my back to anyone. Too much could happen when you're not looking.

Once the waitress comes to take my order, I ask for water and a grilled chicken sandwich with a side salad. I have to repeat my order twice because she keeps getting distracted.

Normally I'd be all over her, using my looks to get what I want. But I'm not feeling it tonight. It's just annoying me right now.

She finally gets it right and stumbles away when a group of people comes to sit at the table exactly opposite of mine.

I see a man that's of average height, a woman with red hair, and a girl with chestnut brown hair. It comes down to the middle of her back. She is turned so I can't get a good look at her.

Watching the group of people while I eat, I can't help but feel invested in them. It's as if I've known them my whole life. I feel drawn in by the brunette especially. There is something familiar about her.

There is a gust of wind that blows the brunettes napkin over. She turns to pick it up and if I wasn't sitting down, I'd have collapsed. My legs turn to jello. The ground below me starts to shake, and I have to grab onto the table to keep from falling over in my chair. Only I quickly realize the ground is not shaking. It's all in my head.

My pulse is racing. I can feel the pounding of my heart inside of my head. I'm worried I'm about to have a heart attack as my chest tightens. I feel my breathing catch in my lungs. I've forgotten how to breathe and it's all because of this woman. This woman that I've never met but somehow knew she existed my whole life. This woman that has been seated at a table just a few feet ahead of me. I need to get a closer look. I don't just want to be closer to her, I physically feel the pull to be closer. I have no other choice. She has been my reason for living.

Leaning forward, I grab my glass of water and take a huge gulp. My throat is a desert, and I need this woman to quench the thirst. Dropping three twenties into the table, I make my way toward the brunette.

I want to watch her. I want to learn everything about her. I'm desperate to know what she likes and what she hates. I need to give her everything. I need to touch her, but I can't.

Leaving the table that was holding me captive, I walk to the other side of the outdoor patio. It's a lot busier now, so I take the barstool along the barrier. It allows me to get a clear view of my brunette.

Her cheeks are flushed from the wine she is drinking. Her hair flows around her face as she laughs. Tucking that lush hair behind her ears as she laughs has me growing hard. I don't care who sees me right now. She is the only one that matters to me, and she can't see me from this angle.

Part of me wants to go claim what is now mine, but there is no way my girl is ready for that. She looks so innocent. She has no idea what I have planned for her. My girl.

My girl.

Is she my one? Is she the one I've been looking for?

I can't help but look at her more intently. Learning every millimeter of her face. The way her right eyebrow arches when she is confused. The way her laugh is soft, but shines over everyone else's. The way her skin looks like buttercream. I bet it's so sweet to taste. Even the cute scrunchie that's around her right hand has me itching to touch it.

The way her hazel eyes sparkle in the moonlight has my dick throbbing. It's pressing against the zipper of my pants. It's starting to hurt, but I don't look away.

The waitress across the way drops a handful of silverware. People look and go back to what they were doing. Everyone except my one, that is. She gets out of her chair so fast and helps the poor woman pick it up. She's so caring

When she reaches for a fork that has fallen under the table, I get a view of her lower back. God help me. A moan releases from my lips, but thankfully no one hears it over the music playing.

What I would give to have my hands on her. Just one touch. Just one brush would tide me over.

Just as I finish my thought, she stands up and heads inside of the restaurant. Maybe she is using the restroom. Even having her out of my sight for one minute has my heart aching.

Unable to lose sight of her, I follow her into the restaurant. I flow through the crowd like a blade cutting cake. She's fast for a little thing.

I see her dip into the bathroom, so I stop at the bar and order a drink. It takes every ounce of control I have to not break down that door just to be near her. I have waited so long for her, I can't let her go.

When she finally emerges from the restroom, I grab my drink and sip on it as I watch her pass. The smell of her scent engulfs me. I want to bathe in that smell, her smell.

I'd give up everything I owned just for one brush of her lips against mine. Is this what Rachel was talking about? Love at first sight? If so, then call me a believer because I'm in love.

She takes a seat back at the table with her friends, but then, the guy touches her shoulder and smiles.

I will break off his damn fingers.

She shrugs his hands off. Good job Princess . That hand doesn't belong on you. Only mine belong on you! Soon you will know that. Soon you will burn for my touch.

They all start to get up and leave. Panic runs through me. I'm not ready for her to leave. I need more time.

Ditching my drink, I cross her path. Just as she walks by, I brush her arm ever so slightly. As we graze by each other, I quickly pull the scrunchie off of her arm. I do it so fast, she doesn't even notice.

I pause in the middle of the restaurant. Not caring who sees me, I lift the hair scrunchie to my nose and smell her.

Fuck me.

She smells like flowers and vanilla, and it's the most engulfing smell I've ever known. I have to force myself not to grab myself because my dick is begging for attention. Her attention.

I turn back and watch her leave. I hate that I don't know her name. I hate that I'm not leaving with her. I hate knowing she won't be in my bed tonight. Is she even going home? I hate that I don't know.

I finally found her, and I have to watch her walk away. I have to fight every fiber in my body, every atom in me not to take her tonight. I want to lock her in my house and never let her out, but I can't do that to her. She is special. I have to treat her as such. She's a little kitten. I have to wait until she is ready or she will be skittish.

Turning on my heels, I follow her for a while. Her and her friends get into a small car and drive off.

She's gone and I'm pissed. I'm pissed and hard as a rock. I need to sink myself into my kitten, but I can't.

Jumping into my truck, I send Zeak a text. I tell him to find the name and address of my dark haired princess. Then, I drive to the one woman I can bend over without saying a word to.

As soon as I reach Rachel's apartment, I run straight up to her door. She better be awake or I'll be pounding on the door until she answers.

Sure, I could find some chick to fuck real fast, but that may take an hour to get her skirt up. Rachel is only a ten minutes drive down the road, and I need a release now. My dick is harder than it's ever been, and It's starting to hurt.

She answers on the second knock. Dressed in an oversized shirt and short shorts, her eyes go wide when she sees me. I'm guessing she wasn't expecting me. I'm sure she now thinks I'm here to apologize, to say I was wrong and I do love her.

Oh no Beauty. I'm sorry, but I found my one. I'm just here to use you.

I grab her throat and shove her backwards. If someone saw this, they would probably think I was breaking in and call the cops. I don't stop there because I'm desperate. All I see is red right now.

Closing my eyes, I kiss Rachel hard. My lips are like stone. I crash against hers, butting her teeth against mine as I do. It hurts, but I don't care. I hold my eyes closed as I picture my brunette princess. I don't have a name, but I will soon. And soon, I'll have her.

"Ouch. Conrad, what are you doing?" Rachel's cry is muffled because I don't let up. Her hands fly up to my hand as it tightens around her neck. She pulls at it. I haven't blocked off her airway, but her body is panicking as if I did. I'm sure her head is getting woozy from the loss of blood flow.

No, I don't want her to pass out, but I want her to calm the fuck down. I want her to surrender to me to make this easier. I want her to let me use her because that's what I want. Because that's what I desire.

Breaking the kiss and loosening my grip on her, I shove my hand down the front of her shorts. "Be my good beauty, and open up for me," I say to her as I circle her swollen little nub. She might have been surprised and scared, but her body was enjoying it.

I imagine the way my girl feels. I bet she will get even wetter for me. I bet her legs will shake at the mer touch of my fingers. She is going to be a vision without even trying.

Shoving a finger into her slick folds, I feel the vibrations of her moan as she grinds against me. She's being greedy. She wants more. Sorry, it's not about you anymore. It's about her.

Removing my fingers from her aching pussy, I pull her shorts down to her ankles. "Step out of them, now." Without thought, she obeys.

At least she is good at taking orders. I bet my girl will be such a good princess.

Pulling my dick out, I roll a condom onto it with shaky hands. I'm on edge, and I've never felt so out of control before. I'm always level headed and clear minded, but not right now. Not since I saw her. Not since I sniffed the scrunchie. Not since I watched her drive away.

Turning her around, I slid into her with a little extra force. Like the last time, I'm not thinking of Rachel. This time I'm thinking of my girl. I can picture her face. Her silk skin and the way her brown hair falls over her shoulder.

I can't wait to wrap my hand around that hair and pull on it while I fuck her into oblivion.

Soon Princess. Soon.

Grabbing a handful of brown hair, I picture her. I hold onto Rachel's hair as if it's a feather to my one, as if it's a lifeline that will bring me closer to her right now. It's a connection. A bond.

I can hear Rachel screaming and grabbing onto the bookshelf. My fingers dig into her hips. She will definitely have bruises tomorrow. She will like the memory, but then again, maybe she won't.

Pushing into her deeper, I need more. I can feel my release begging to let go. It's so close I can feel it about to spill over the edge. It's so close it burns, but it won't come. I won't cum, and it's because I need her. I need my one.

Pulling out of her in one swift motion I grab her hair and shove her onto the couch. I'm not sweet to her. I don't care if it hurts her. She will be fine. She is getting pleasure from it too. She just may walk around with a few more bruises than usual.

Once I have her on the couch, I lay her flat on her back. Hoping the deeper angle helps me get off, I slam into her. Over and over and over. Not wanting to see her face, I place my whole hand over her face and stick my thumb in her mouth so she can't talk. All I see is brown hair. This could be my girl under me. I hear her moan as she starts to suck on my thumb, but it's not enough.

Frustration flows over me as I hear my phone ring. Looking at my watch, I see it's Zeak. "Fuck." I pull out of Rachel, and she cries from the loss of my dick. I don't bother looking at her. I already know she is pouting. I can hear her huff and puff.

"You better have something," I curse at the phone. I'm sure Rachel thinks I'm pissed off because I had to stop fucking her, but really I'm pissed off because I haven't been able to get off.

"Yeah. I found her name and address. I will send it to you now. Anything else you need from me?" Zeak asks, getting right to business. I like that about him. No pleasantries. Why would I need them?

"That's all. Thanks." I hang up as fast as I possibly can, because I need to know who my one is. I need to know her name and where she lives.

Annabell Brown.

I read her name over and over again. It's sweat on my tongue. I can't wait to say it out loud. I can't wait to have her name roll off my tongue as I come down her throat. My girl. Mine.

Annabell Brown. You don't know it yet, but you're already mine.

Chapter 10 Conrad

I can't leave Rachel's apartment fast enough. My feet are flying off the pavement. "Why are you leaving?" Rachel yells at me as I tuck my hard dick back into my jeans which hurts. I still can't find a release, but I have to see Annabell.

My Annabell.
My one.
My Princess.
Mine.

"Work. I have to go." I rush out the door with no explanation. I'm sure I've hurt her feelings, but she will get over it. She's a grown girl. She knows work is important. And tonight is the most important work I've ever done in my life.

I'm sure Rachel will still be pissed come Monday morning. I'll deal with that later.

I've never driven my truck so fast. My wheels screech at every turn I make thanks to the rain. Annabell's place is about fifteen miles away, and I cannot get there fast enough.

It's as if I don't get there right away I'll die. Though, I might because I can't seem to breathe at the moment. I'm holding my breath for reasons unknown. It's a waste of time right now.

Pulling into her apartment complex, my stomach does flips. I can't remember the last time I was this nervous and excited about something…about someone.

I hear my phone buzz. Pulling out my phone to see if it's Zeak with any new information. I regret it immediately.

Rachel: What the hell Conrad?

I ignore her.

"Apartment 314, where are you?" I ask out loud. As soon as I spot her apartment, I pull into the closest spot.

Scanning the apartments and the area, I'm pissed. This place is a dump and that's being nice about it.

Why do you live here Princess?

You need me more than you know.

I'll take care of her as soon as I can.

Sitting in my truck, I watch. I have a clear shot into her living room and her bedroom, but I don't see her.

She really needs to close those blinds. I don't want anyone else to see her.

My phone goes off again and I roll my eyes when I see it's Rachel. I don't even bother reading her text.

Movement. I see someone move inside her apartment. I jerk up, and lean over the steering wheel. Trying to get a better look, I clean off my windshield. The wipers and fluid allow me to see my girl perfectly.

She is dressed in a pink crop t-shirt and black athletic shorts.

Fuck.

She looks too good. She needs to cover up before I take that as an invitation and break down the fucking door. I'm sure it wouldn't be difficult. It looks like a piece of plywood.

I look down at my arm to see her pink scrunchie still on my wrist. Even after fucking Rachel, it's still there. It matches her pink crop top. I wonder if she misses it?

Maybe I should return it to you. Would you like that?

I watch as climbs into her bed. She crawls and on her stomach with her legs bent and ankles in the air.

If only I could be between those legs.

Watching as she rocks her ankles back and forward mindlessly, I feel my dick grow.

Here we go again.

I'm not sure how I'm going to survive on the sidelines. Not with the way she unknowingly teases me.

I can see her shorts ride up with every flick of her ankle. Her ass is begging for me to touch it. To leave a bright red handprint on her. I'm not sure if I want to hurt her or comfort her.

Could I have both?

Pulling out my dick, I start to rub it slowly. The image of her, so innocent, so naïve, makes me not only pulsate but it makes me excited to take that innocence from her.

As I pick up my speed, the pink scrunchie rubs against my dick. The friction makes me crave more. Taking it off my wrist, I slide it over my dick.

Settling nice and snug around the base of my dick, I smile. The image of Annabell's scrunchie around my dick is almost enough to make me come right there. It's fucking dirty, and I love it.

Pumping myself as I watch Annabell roll over and watch TV, I get a clear view of her pussy. Unfortunately, it's covered with her shorts, but I imagine it bare for me.

Grabbing the steering wheel with my left hand, because I feel like I'm about to lose control. My right hand pumps faster, hitting the scrunchie every time.

Just as I'm about to find my release, she stands up and walks over towards the window. She stares out and I cum all over my hand. Cum runs down my hand as I let out a loud moan.

Fuck, Annabell.

I don't even worry about cleaning up. I just hold my aching dick as I watch her. She stares outside looking around. Is she looking for me? Does she feel my gaze? Then, she closes the blinds and she's gone.

Composing myself, I clean off my hand and pull the scrunchie back around my wrist. Thankfully, it didn't get too messy.

I'll be back for you tomorrow, Princess.

I headed straight here from Annabell's. I wanted to do something to commemorate me finding my one.

"You ready?" The body piercer asks. I nod because I've been ready! I've been dying to get my nipples pierced for years. It's a sign of strength. They did this in the ancient times to signify power. Now that I found her, I can get them.

With her, I'm stronger. With her, I'm whole. She is my strength. With her I'm even more powerful. Without her, I was a deflated version of myself. Once I have her in my arms, everything will have been worth it.

The needle goes into my sensitive nipples. I relish the pain because I feel pleasure from it. I have to be careful not to get hard from it while I think of Annabell. Wouldn't want to excite the body piercer.

My phone buzzes in my pocket and I pull it out to see who it is. Of course, it's Rachel.

Rachel: Why are you ignoring me?

That's exactly what I do. I ignore her.

Standing proudly, I look at my chest in the mirror. They look fucking awesome! "Thanks," I say as I pull my shirt and jacket back on. Handing her a hundred dollar bill, I walk back out to my truck.

It's close to midnight now, so I need to get back to the house and give her medicine. She has been reacting poorly to the current medication, so I have to find something else. I'm no doctor, so this may take some time.

It's probably the perfect time to part ways with Rachel. I'll help her get a new job because I'm not a complete dick. But I don't want Rachel to get in the way of Annabell. She is my first priority.

Zeak sent me a file on Annabell while I was getting my piercings. Hopefully this will give me some insight on my next step.

I want to dive into the email he sent, but I have to get home and deal with Barbara. Now I feel like it was a waste of time and energy taking over Barbara's life.

The only issues I've had with her are a few missed doctors appointments. I had to convince them that I was her estranged nephew. Thankfully, they didn't ask too many questions because she's actually an only child.

Idiots.

Arriving home, I give Barbara her sleeping medicine and head to my office. Opening my laptop, I immediately go to Zeaks email.

Annabell Jade Brown. There is a picture of her in what looks like scrubs.

Fuck you're perfect.

Why is she in scrubs? I couldn't possibly get that lucky. Could I?

Scrolling through the email, I speed read all the important info.

-Only child
-From California
-Type A+
-LPN license
-Date of birth

Fuck she is young.

Seriously? That has to be a typo. If not, I'm the luckiest guy out there. I mean seriously, what are the odds she is also a nurse?

I picture her working here and helping me with Barbara, but I don't want her to go home to that shit hole. I want her to stay here. Maybe this could be a live-in position. We would both benefit from that.

I feel my phone buzz. Reaching into my pocket as fast as possible, I check. It might be Zeak with more info. It's not.

Rachel: Conrad. I need to hear from you.

Not right now woman.

I could keep an eye on her while I wait for her to fall in love with me, and I could give her a job she can't refuse.

But how do I make her quit her job?

No one would quit their job to go stay with a stranger, unless she is desperate.

Pulling out my phone, I send a quick text to Zeak.

Conrad: Get Annabell fired from her job. Like tomorrow.

Zeak: Alright? How do you want me to do that?

Conrad: That's your fucking job to figure out.

Zeak: On it.

I want her here tonight. I hate the thought of her in that apartment by herself. So unprotected. So vulnerable. So helpless.

My dick starts to get hard once again as I think about watching her, breaking into her apartment, and crawling into her bed.

Soon my Princess. Soon.

Chapter 11 Conrad

I wait as the rain continues to pelt down on me. Lost in thought, I feel my phone vibrate. Pulling out my phone, I see a text from Rachel. Taking a deep breath I prepare myself as I read.

Rachel: All we ever do anymore is fuck. Do you not want more?

Rachel: Don't ignore me or I'll keep blowing your phone up.

Well I can't say I didn't expect this. I seriously don't have time for this right now, but I guess it's time I answer her. I can't ignore her forever.

Maybe she's doing me a favor. She's being crazy which gives me a way out, and Annabell a way in.

Conrad: No I don't want more.

Yeah, I'm about to be a dick. I could be nice about it, but then she won't leave on her own.

Rachel: You're kidding me right now!

Conrad: I'm not much for jokes.

Rachel: Don't do this.

Rachel: I can't lose you.

Fuck. I thought she'd be easy to get rid of. I should have known better. How is she so clingy already?

Conrad: We just aren't meshing well.

Rachel: How? We can make this work.

Conrad: Just let it go. I'm not interested in doing that.

Rachel: You're just scared of love. You're pushing me away because you love me too.

What is this woman's problem? She seriously thinks I love her? I can't get away from her fast enough. I guess I'll have to be even more of an ass.

Conrad: I don't love you. I don't want to be with you. This is done!

She texts back right away.

Rachel: Screw you Conrad. You will regret this. I promise you that. I quit.

And there it is. That's exactly what I wanted from you, Rachel. Thank you, it took long enough though.

I don't respond because I don't want to. All I want to do is find my girl. It's been hours since I last saw her, and it's making me insane.

Looking at my watch, I realize she is late. Annabell should have come through here by now. She gets off work, and walks this exact street to get home. I itch to be near her. My body is aching with the absence of her. I'm already obsessed, and I haven't even gotten a taste yet.

Just as I shove my phone back into my pocket, I see her. She is running.

Why are you running, Princess? Do you not like the rain? Do you not like getting wet? You better get used to it because from the moment we meet, you will never stop being wet for me.

I place myself right in her path, and she crashes right into me. I'm hardly affected, but she bounces off me like a bouncy ball. She lands on her back and her bag hits the sidewalk beside her.

I can't help but stare as her hair cascades around her beautiful, fair skin. Our eyes lock for the first time, and I swear magic happens. The sun pushes through the clouds allowing me to get a better look at her. I'm not sure how it's possible, but she is even more radiant.

She looks at me as if she is a deer in headlights. It's jaw clenching. Her lips part and shut just as quickly. I can't help but study her, and it makes a grin slip through.

What are you thinking, Princess?

Bending down to get level with her, she draws me in. I can't help but get closer to her. Every atom in my body wants to grab her and ravish her, but I can't. To her, we are strangers. But soon we won't be. Soon, you will be mine.

She is just inches from me, and all I can think about is tasting those lips. She is staring at me as if she wants me to. I can smell her floral perfume, and it's driving me crazy. I'd be surprised if she couldn't see how hard I am already. "Are you alright?" I ask before I give in to my ache for her.

I wait for her response, but she just stares at me. Maybe I affect her as much as she affects me, or she hit her head and is seeing stars.

I'd love to make you see stars, Princess.

The thought makes me smile again. Damn my imagination. My smile fades as she nods her head.

Good. At least I know she can hear me.

Extending my hand, I beg her to accept my offer. She watches my arms as if it's a new object she has never seen before.

Is she admiring me? I like the thought of that.

My muscles twitch at the anticipation. I'm waiting with my arm extended, but she is lost in her thoughts.

Grab my hand, Princess. Let me feel you for the first time.

With shaky hands, she grabs my hand. As soon as she does, her cheeks go red. I try so hard not to let my mind go wild, but I can't help but wonder if her ass cheeks would be as red after I spanked her?

No, she isn't ready for that yet.

Pulling her to her feet, I watch her for a few more moments. "Take it easy," I force from my lips. Unable to help myself, I allow myself one more touch. Placing my hand on the small of her back, I steady her before I walk off into the crowd of people. Both cursing and praising myself, I wait to turn back and watch her as she jogs closer towards her apartment.

"Nice job Zeak," I say into the phone Sunday morning. He did his job and got her fired. I guess her company has a "three strikes and you're out" policy. So he sent in three complaints and made it look like it was from the families she is assisting.

"Anything else you need?" He asks in his bored voice. As if his work is so easy he needs a challenge.

"Did you get that "Help Wanted" sign posted?

"I sure did, boss. Got it up last night," Zeak says, proud of himself.

"Good, that's it for now then." We both hang up and go back to our work.

I subconsciously play with my newly pierced nipple rings. The pain feels good. It reminds me of my Annabell, and how she will soon be here, with me, under my protection…possession.

I had him post a "Help Wanted" sign on the billboard by her running trail. Now, all I have to do is wait and hope she sees it.

Abandoning my work, I grab my hoodie and head to my truck. I have to see her. Who knows what she is doing? Who knows if she is seeking comfort in someone else since she lost her job. She better not be. I'll end every last one of them.

As soon as I pull up to her apartment I see her outside with her dog. It reminds me of Rox. I sure miss him. He had a good life, except for that one day.

"Anna-banana, what a coincidence. We are both outside at the same time. Are you going for a run? That's so cool. I should start running," I hear someone say just as I roll my windows down.

They can't see me. I'm blocked by a tree, but I can see them clearly. I can see a guy stepping closer to Annabell.

Who the fuck is that guy? And why is he talking to my girl?

I know why he is talking to her. She is breathtaking, but she is also mine. Her hair is put up in a lazy pony tail. It would be perfect for grabbing and controlling her with.

She ducks her head and runs off. I can't be sure if she said anything, but it looks as if she doesn't enjoy his company.

Good.

I watch her ass as it bounces when she runs. It teases me. It wants my hands on it. It wants my touch. It just doesn't know it yet, neither does she. She will soon enough though.

Fifteen minutes go by, and I still haven't received an email from her. I know I'm being impatient. She is running with her older dog, it's going to take longer to reach the board. Unable to help myself, I start down the trail. Jogging at a fast pace, I reach the board in five minutes.

Immediately spotting her, I pretend to rest and enjoy the view. Although, I don't have to pretend to enjoy this view. She lets her dog roam as she scans the billboard. I can tell the moment she sees the flyer. Her body tenses up, and she rips it off the board.

That's my girl.

I watch as she pulls out her phone and types away. She better be emailing me. Thankfully, two minutes later I feel my phone buzz.

Opening my email, I smile.

To whom it may concern,

I am interested in your available position. I am an LPN. I am great with the elderly as I have two years of experience, and I can start right away. I can provide references if needed. I have attached my resume to this email. I look forward to hearing from you.

Thank you for this opportunity.

Annabell Brown

    Finally! I have you exactly where I want you, on the hook. Now, I just need to reel you in.

    It takes Annabell twenty minutes to get back to her apartment. I give her a big head start, and take in a deep breath as I pass her just before her apartment complex comes into view.
    Jumping into my truck, I watch her carry her dog as she slowly walks up to her door and unlocks it. Already missing her, I pull out my phone and send a reply. I honestly couldn't wait any longer. My fingers were itching to respond.

Dear Ms. Annabell Brown,

We would love to have you come in for an interview. How is tomorrow at 9am?

If this time works for you let me know as soon as you can. I have several meetings planned for tomorrow.

Conrad King

I hate to admit it, but I watch my phone and wait for her response. It does not come, and it's starting to piss me off the longer I have to wait.

What are you doing in there?

Unable to wait, my curiosity gets the better of me. Jumping out of the truck, I walk up to her apartment. I can see her in her living room on the couch. It's been almost thirty minutes since I replied.

As I peer in, I see her hair is wet. It makes me feel a little less annoyed knowing she was probably in the shower most of this time. My anger subsides, but arousal quickly takes its place. Thinking of her in the shower makes my dick harden to the point of discomfort.

Watching her grab her phone, I can help but smile when I see the shocked look on her face. Her fingers move so fast, it takes her no time to reply to my email.

Mr. King,

I appreciate the quick response. I would love to come by at 9am.

Thank you so much! I look forward to it.

Annabell Brown

That's my girl. I will see you soon.

Even though I reply to her email while I watch her on her couch, I wait fifteen minutes until I hit send.

Ms. Annabell Brown,

Arrive right at 9am tomorrow. Park on the east side of the house. There is a door to the left of the garage. You may enter through there. I will meet you in the kitchen.

1361 Stone Kings Court, Seattle

Conrad King

    To my liking, she watches her phone in hope for an email. That's exactly how I want you, Annabell. Waiting for me.

Mr. King,

I will be there right at 9am. Thank you for the instructions and thank you for the opportunity. I look forward to meeting with you.

Annabell Brown

    Oh, I look forward to you meeting me too. I can't wait to see the look on your face when you see me. I can't wait to smell that floral perfume up close again, and possibly touch you again.
    Not much longer Annabell. Not much longer.

Chapter 12 Conrad

"You're killing me, Annabell," I say with a growl as I watch her on the cameras. She's trying her hardest to keep that skirt of hers from flying up. I bite my knuckles when I see her pink panties as her skirt flies up. My dick starts to grow just thinking what it would be like to have those panties between my teeth.

I can't help but laugh as she looks around to see if anyone has seen her.

Oh I see you, Princess.

Barbara has been the bane of my existence. All I want to do is focus on Annabell, but she has been demanding my attention. If I didn't need her, I would have done away with her by now. I've been struggling with her medication. Too bad I'm not a medical doctor. It would make all of this much easier. Apparently, the medication I've been giving her is making her blood pressure and pulse rise. I can't have her stroking out on me right now. Then, there would be no reason for Annabell to stay.

I hear the softest knock on the side door. If I wasn't aware of Annabell's presence, I probably would have missed the knock. "Come in." I try my hardest not to sound too eager. I want to drag her inside and hold her in my arms, but I can't. I have to wait.

I watch her the whole time she walks down the hallway. She can't see me because her eyes are on the floor making sure she doesn't trip. She is nervous for the interview.

Just wait until you see who is about to interview you, Princess.

She trots down the hallway as if she is crawling through it. She isn't graceful by any means, but she is absolute perfection.

This is going to be fun. "Ms. Annabell Brown I presume?" I stick my hand out to shake hers. I act as if she is just another one of my interviewees and not the woman I'm obsessed with.

It's her. She is actually sitting in the kitchen with me. I can't take my eyes off of her.

"Yes, that's me," she says with a sour face. The moment her hand touches mine, I can feel myself get a little tighter in the trousers.

This interview is going to be much more difficult than I imagined.

"Conrad King. It's nice to meet you," I say as my jaw clenches. I'm trying my best to control myself, but it's almost impossible with her. I've never met anyone like her. As I slowly release her hand, I can't help but slightly brush my thumb over her fingers. They are incredibly soft.

I wonder where else you're that soft?

For some reason, she has yet to speak since I introduced myself.

Is she pissed?

"I'm so glad you could come on such short notice. I need to hire someone as soon as possible," I inform her. I hope she is ready to move in because I can't wait any longer. It's been torture not having her under my roof.

"I'm pleased to be here. I can make that work. I am able to start right away." She gives me a forced smile, but I can tell she isn't very happy.

What is the matter, Annabell?

I want to pull her into my arms and force her scowl into a moan.

"Perfect. Let's do this then," I say as I pull out the keys in my pocket. They slip around in my hands. My hands twitch to touch her, so much so, they fumble the keys. I can tell she is confused, so I continue.

"How is nine am tomorrow morning?" I slide into the barstool next to her. I try to keep my distance, even though ever thing in me is yelling at me to, "Just fucking kiss her."

"Nine am tomorrow for what?" She questions me with a raised eyebrow.

"For work." I raise my eyebrow back at her.

Does she not want the job? I thought she was desperate. Have I misread the situation?

"I'm sorry, are you hiring me?"

I can't help but smile at her uncertainty. Fuck me, I'm rewarded with the biggest smile as soon as I nod, but it fades just as quickly.

What happened, Princess?

"Do you want the job?" I try my hardest to hide my concern because I'm not sure what I would do if she said no.

"Oh, I do. I just thought I'd have to answer some questions and talk about my past work experience. Maybe take a look around and meet the woman I will be taking care of." She rambles on, but I couldn't care less about any other details. I guess I should play the part though.

"You have your license, correct?" She nods. "And you have experience?" She nods again. "Then I think we are good here."

I can see her mind working overtime. I want to tell her to stop overthinking things, but she speaks up before I can. "And what are the keys for?"

Shit, I forgot to tell her it was a live-in position. That better not be a deal breaker or I will tie you to the fucking banister, Annabell.

"They are to the house and to the bedroom you will be living in," I say with a nod. I'm hoping if I act as if it's no big deal then she will think it's no big deal. Not sure I'll be getting that lucky though.

"Oh, I didn't realize this was a live-in position. I have a dog that lives with me. I'm sure you don't want a dog in this beautiful house." She looks around and shrugs.

Is she trying to get out of this? Not going to happen.

"The dog is fine. Just don't let her get in the way of your work." I try my best to look unsure because of course I know she has a dog.

"My mother is down this hall to my right. She is comatose. She will not be a bother, but she requires 'round-the-clock care, as she needs meds delivered to her during the night as well. You will be nicely compensated for this," I try to reassure her.

I can tell she is still thinking. I'm sure she is wondering if she can trust me. Can she live in a mansion with a complete stranger? I watch as her eyes go wide.

"Do you live on the premises?"

"I do," I say with a smirk. Yes, Princess. You will be right down the hall from me. Just the way I want you.

I picture her sleeping in her room that will be next to mine. Does she sleep on her side? On her back? On her stomach so I can sneak in and fuck her without her knowing it's me. What will she wear? Does she sleep naked? Fuck I pray she does.

I can see the hesitation in her eyes, and I can't have that. "Is that a problem, Ms. Annabell?" I reach over and tuck a piece of her hair behind her ears. I can feel her shake under my touch.

Damn it. Her hair is like silk under my finger tips. I don't want to release her, but I do.

"Um, no," she says nervously, but that's alright. We will fix that nervousness soon enough.

"Great! I will show you to your room. You can start moving your stuff in tonight. I will need you to start working tomorrow," I say, knowing it's a lie. She can't start tomorrow because Barbars meds still haven't arrived. They won't arrive until next week, but I want her here now.

Zeak found me some meds that shouldn't affect her blood pressure as much. It's called Pentobarbital. I honestly don't care what it is, as long as it keeps her asleep and gives Annabell a reason to be here.

"You live close by, right?" I ask, but then realize I probably shouldn't have said that. Even though I know it is a fact.

"How did you know that?" She asks after she nods.

"Lucky guess." I give her a wink to distract her. Her cheeks go red and it makes my dick jerk.

Oh Annabell, we're about to get into so much trouble.

"I will be back in a few hours Mr. King," she says as she heads back down the hallway.

She seems eager, good. I like that.

"Please, call me Conrad," I say through gritted teeth. I don't want to hear her call me a made up name. One day, I'll hear her call my full name, but for now, just my first name will have to do.

She twists her fingers when she turns around. "Yes, Sir."

Fuck. I can feel my dick stirring. It's ready to go, and I'm having a hell of a time hiding it from her. I'm going to be so sore from being so hard. I want nothing more than for her to call me Sir, but if she keeps doing that I'll end up ripping her clothes off before it's time. I can't help but look at her with fire in my eyes. She doesn't realize what she has just said.

I want this girl to say "Yes, Sir." I want her to do it while she is on her knees crawling towards me. While she is bent over the island. While I'm pouring my come into her.

"I'm sorry. I meant, Conrad. Can I at least call you Mr. Conrad?" She says, pulling me from my dark thoughts. It's probably best.

"Alright," I nod. You can call me that for now, Princess.

"Thank you. Sorry, I feel more comfortable calling you 'mister'. It has nothing to do with your age. Not that you're old. I don't think that at all. I mean, look at you. Not that I'm looking at you. Gosh, no. That's definitely not it, Sir. Oh whoops. Sorry again. I meant Mr. Conrad. It's just because you're my employer. Sorry."

I watch as she covers that luscious mouth with her hand. As if that's the only way to stop her from babbling on. I let a laugh slip out. I can see her cheeks redden, and I can't help but love how I make her nervous.

"I'm sorry. I ramble when I'm nervous," she admits. My smile lingers, but all humor vanishes.

"Why are you nervous, Ms. Annabell Brown?"

"I um, you make me a little nervous." Of course I do, Princess. "I do?" My grin widens uncontrollably. Maybe she will be easier to make mine than I thought. It seems I already affect her.

"I mean, I'm nervous for the job interview," I hear her talking, but I lose focus. She reaches up and plays with her bottom lip. It has my dick stirring. The way she rolls it between her fingers has me glaring hard. I want to roll that lip between my teeth.

"I have to pack a lot if I am going to get everything moved tonight," she finishes as she walks backwards. Tripping over nothing, I want to reach out for her, but she catches herself before I get there. I can't help but chuckle as she quickly flees.

It's been an hour since she left, and I can't get our meeting out of my head. I need to focus on installing the rest of these cameras before she gets back, but I have to pause every few minutes because my dick is straining against my jeans and it hurts like hell.

I make her nervous. Good. I like that. Her little ramble was the cutest thing I've ever heard. She couldn't stop, and I sure as hell wasn't going to stop her. Watching her biting her lip in panic made my dick jump.

I'm glad she doesn't think I'm old. That would have been an issue. But if she had, I would just have to show her what experience will do for you. I'm sure by the end of it, she wouldn't think I was old. But by her reaction, I can tell she is attracted to me. Hopefully she will be back soon. She will be right where she belongs. With me.

Just as I'm putting the last camera in Annabell's room, my phone alarm goes off. "Shit." I jump off the ladder and run down the stairs as fast as possible. The alarm that went off on my phone was not a reminder alarm. It was a trigger alarm I set up for any kind of movement in Barbara's room. If anything moves in there, the alarm goes off.

That can only mean one thing. Barbara is awake.

Chapter 13 Annabell

I got the job! I still can't believe this. After packing and calling my mom to tell her the news, I rush back over to the mansion. I can't help but get anxious to see Mr. Conrad again. I'm not sure what it is about him, but he makes me nervous.

Walking up to the side door I entered through a few hours ago, I wonder if I should use the key I was given, or should I knock? I guess he wouldn't have given me a key if he didn't intend on me using it. I go to turn the knob, and I'm thankful it's still unlocked.

"Hello," I whisper. I'm not sure why I whisper. I actually want him to hear me. I tiptoe down the same hall to the kitchen. My curiosity gets the better of me as I walk deeper into the house. Just past the kitchen door is the grand living room, and boy is it grand. Five of my apartments could fit inside this one room alone.

I let my eyes run over the beauty that is this mansion. Continuing my exploration, I turn the corner still following the hallway that leads behind the grand living room. He said his mother's room was down the hall. I walk even quieter as I reach the end of the hallway.

"Hello," I whisper again. I'm not sure why I do. Mr. Conrad said she was comatose.

I reach my hand to the doorknob, and all of a sudden it swings open. I let out a small scream and cover my mouth. It's Mr. Conrad. He pops out of the room so fast it scared me half to death. He quickly shuts the door behind him.

"Ms. Annabell, you're here." His eyes are wide with surprise.

"Is that ok? I have all my things in my car."

He places his hand on the small of my back and leads me back into the living room. Just that small touch from him gives me shivers. Unfortunately, I think he notices, but he pretends not to.

I see a smile take over his face. I don't think I'm supposed to though. "Absolutely. I'm glad you're here. The sooner we get you all settled in the better. Did you say you have all of your things in your car?" He gives me a confused look.

"Well, everything besides the bed and the couch," I say with a little shrug. Obviously I couldn't fit them in my little car.

"You don't have many things then. Come on, I'll show you to your room." He moves his hand towards my side as he ushers me upstairs. Why are we going upstairs? I feel like I should be near his mom.

We walk up the grand staircase slowly. I know I should have so many questions. So many thoughts should be running through my head, but the only thing I can think of is his hand on me. It hasn't left my back since the hallway.

Should I tell him to move? Should I nonchalantly side step him so it drops off my back? I should do both of these things, but I don't. My body won't let me.

Once we reach the top of the staircase he slowly drops his hand from my side, and I swear I pout for a moment. I was getting used to the heat his hand was bringing to the small of my back. There might have been some heat coming from another place too if we are being completely honest.

Jeez, Anne. I mentally slap myself for thinking that. *This is your employer. You cannot think of him like that! No matter how pantie droppingly gorgeous he is.*

"Your room is the second door on the left." He gestures at the door. This massive staircase leading down an open hallway that overlooks the grand living room. I could get used to this.

"You have the only key to this room. It's the silver one on your keychain." He points to me signaling I need to open the door.

"Oh, right." I fumble with the key. Once I get it in the keyhole, I open the door slowly. Not sure what I'm expecting, but it definitely wasn't this. This bedroom is bigger than my apartment. No joke. The bed is placed diagonally to the right of me. Across from the bed is another door. I assume that is the closet.

Is that a tub? Sure enough, there is a beautiful black, claw foot tub in the back left corner. Why on earth would you need a tub in your bedroom?

I look back over to the bed. Is that a king? It looks even bigger than that. Maybe it's a California king. I've never seen one in person before. What am I going to do with all that space? Five other people could sleep in it with me. My thoughts drift to Mr. Conrad in bed with me. *No, no, no; stop right now.*

"How do you like it?" Mr. Conrad wakes me from my inappropriate daydream.

"It's amazing. I love it." He walks into the bedroom and sits on the bed. *Good Lord. That's not helping.* I linger in the doorway a little longer than normal. There is awkward silence for what feels like hours.

He stands up and walks towards me. "You can come in. I won't bite," he says as he brushes past me to leave. "Unless you want me to," he whispers in my ear and walks away.

Did that just happen? I'm completely shocked. Surely I didn't hear him correctly. I don't know if I should be running for the hills or begging him to stay in my room.

Before I lose my mind and ask him to stay, I spin around and shut the door behind me. *Breathe, Anne. Just breathe.*

Once I gain my composure, I explore my room more. It really is like an apartment. I walk over to open the closet door to my left. To my complete surprise I find it is not just a closet. It is also a spacious bathroom. I can't believe this is where I get to live.

The closet is on the left side and the bathroom is on the right. There is a cute bench in the middle of the two. My clothes are going to look so lonely in this large closet.

Walking into the bathroom, I run my fingers along the granite countertops and look at the mirror. My hair is a little out of place, so I comb it with my fingers.

Then, I see the shower. I can't help but get excited as I step into the shower. "Wow," I say out loud. The walk-in shower is as big as my tiny kitchen was. It's covered in beautiful, classic black and white tiles. At least it looks like tile. I'm sure it's some kind of imported material I've never heard of.

I cannot wait to take a shower in this. That tub looks like it would be fun to soak in. I can't help but imagine what Mr. Conrad would look like in it with me.

Chapter 14 Conrad

The look on her face was too good when I told her I'd bite her if she asked. I couldn't help toying with her. It's too easy. The way her cheeks flush from just one comment, I don't know how I'm going to hold out when all I can think about is pulling her clothes off and fucking her until she agrees to be mine.

It took me several minutes to get Barbara sedated again. Something is going on with her medication, and I'm not liking it. Her heart rate is still sporadic. I seriously can't have her stroking out on me right now. I'll lose Annabell, and that cannot happen.

Making my way down to the office, I close the door behind me. As soon as I reach the desk, I pull out my phone from my pocket. Trying to push back the thoughts of biting Annabell's neck, I call Zeak.

"What can I do for you, boss?" He answers on the first ring.

"Where are we with those meds I requested?" I know he said they won't be in until next week, but I'm hoping for a miracle.

"I'm trying boss. My guy just got out of the hospital. His contact is getting them as we speak, but he is pretty far away. He can only get a little at a time so he doesn't raise suspicions. He doesn't want to lose his job." Zeak says all in one breath.

I want to tell him how much I don't care about that guy's job, but it's wasting my breath. I know Zeak is doing everything he can to get it done. "Keep me updated," I say and hang up.

Opening the desk drawer, I see Rachel's old badge I made for her. Pulling out the folders of Barbara's important documents, I toss it in there. I need to shred that since I won't be needing it anymore.

Pushing thoughts of Barb and Annabell to the back of my mind, I focus on my work. Though Annabell has become my priority, I still own a company that needs my attention.

About an hour into work, I hear my phone buzz. Picking it up, I expect there to be a text, but it's not. It's an alert from one of the cameras. At least it's not the alarm from Barbara's room. Clicking on the highlighted picture, I see Annabell walking downstairs.

"And where do you think you're going, Princess?" I watch as she walks through the living room. Then, she disappears. I have cameras set up in her room, Barbara's room, the hallway to Barbs, the living room, my room, my office, and the kitchen.

I flip to the camera in the kitchen just as I see her speed by. Then, I hear her. For a moment I hope she is coming to find me. For a moment I let my thoughts wander to her in my office, naked. But then, the side door shuts.

She's leaving? Where is she going?

Jumping out of my chair, I grab my keys and head to my truck that's parked in the 4th car garage. It's in a private bay by itself. I don't want her to know what vehicle I drive just yet.

Following her with a car between us, I quickly realize she is going back to her apartment, but why? I arrive just as she opens her apartment door. As I sit and watch the closed window, I can't help but think of the last time I was here. I can still feel my cum running down my dick as I got off to the sight of her.

I can feel my pants start to stretch with the thought. Moving to adjust myself, I freeze when I see someone walking towards Annabell's door.

"Who the fuck are you?"

I take a picture of him and send it to Zeak.

Conrad: Find out everything you can about this guy.

Zeak: On it!

I shove my phone into the dashboard holder I have and watch as Annabell comes out of her door. She quickly heads to her car with her dog in tow. She seems to be nervous. Why?

She opens her car door quickly, and then the fucker grabs her wrist. The blood in my veins instantly boils. He is touching what's mine, and she is scared. I can see it in her eyes.

Without thinking, I reach under my seat and grab the gun I keep stashed there. I know I can't blow his head off in public, but I'm not thinking rationally right now. He is hurting my girl, and you don't get to live after doing that.

"If that dog bites me, it will be the last thing she does," I hear the mother fucker say.

Yup, he has to die.

"Then you should get your fucking hands off me because she will bite you," I hear her yell.

I'm halted in my tracks. I've only gotten one step out of the truck. I'm still holding onto the gun in my right hand and the door handle with my left. The sound of her cursing at him has me growing hard once again.

He lets go of her wrist and bows his head. Maybe she can handle herself, but I'll still be dealing with him later.

"I'm sorry, Anna-banana. I wasn't trying to scare you or your dog. I just didn't want you to leave without me getting your number. I can tell you're moving. I will miss you so much."

Anna-banana? What the hell? He has a pet name for her? He knows her. This isn't the first time she has come in contact with him. Is he an ex? My once growing erection fades quickly at the thought of this guy touching her.

She's mine. Not yours.

"I have to go, Tod," I hear her say.

Good girl. Get away from him.

Hopping back into my truck, I slide the gun back into its holster under the seat. I only keep it there for emergencies. I have never actually killed someone with a gun. That's not in the least bit satisfying. If someone deserves to die, they deserve to die slowly. Let the punishment fit the crime, right?

I watch as she safely pulls away, and I start to relax. My pulse slows, but I still watch the fucker. He takes a few steps forward as if to catch her, but then he stops. After a few minutes he slowly treks back to an apartment right across from her.

Good thing she never has to come back here. My girl is safe, and as the that fucker, he will get what's coming to him. I'll make sure he never touches what's mine again.

Putting my truck in drive, I quickly head back to the mansion. I need to make sure Annabell is alright.

Once I arrive, I pull right into the single bay garage and go searching for Annabell. Walking into the side door, I pause and listen. Trying to hear any sign of her, but I don't.

I'm sure she is hiding in her room after the scare she just had. I want to run upstairs and pull her into my arms, but I can't. I'm not that person for her yet. I long for the day she runs to me when needing shelter. Soon, Annabell. Soon.

Deciding to get some more work done, I head to my office but stop when I see the garage door open just a little.

Peering inside, I see the sexy backside of Annabell. I can't help but watch as she admires all the cars. Then, her attention goes to the locked door that's between the garage bays.

Just as she reaches her hand out to the lock I say, "Can I help you find something, Ms. Annabell?" She jumps and lets out the cutest squeal as she whips her body around.

"Oh my gosh. Mr. Conrad, I'm so sorry. I was actually looking for you." I arch my eyebrow. She was snooping. I'm going to have to keep an eye on her. Not that that will be a problem for me.

"I don't think you would find me in a locked room," I tease her. She twists her fingers as if she is nervous. I fucking love how she gets so nervous around me.

Coming to the conclusion, she isn't going to speak, I continue. "Well, you found me. What can I do for you?" I walk closer to her, visibly making her more nervous with the close proximity.

This is going to be so much fun playing with her.

When I take my last step towards her, her dog barks at me. I quickly stop. People are easy to fight off. I can usually guess their next move, but dogs are different. Her dog is probably still in a protective mood from earlier, so I stay put.

"Haci, no," Annabell says.

"Cute dog. I thought she would be smaller." It's a lie because I know exactly how big she was.

"Oh really? Why is that? It's still okay if she stays here, right?" I can hear panic in her voice.

"Of course, Ms. Annabell."

Watching her dog cautiously, I walk closer towards her. I can't help myself. I need to be close to her.

It takes everything I have not to cup her face and feel her lips drag across mine.

Fuck!

"Let's get you settled in, shall we?"

I usher her out of the garage. Unable to help myself, I place my hand on her mid back. I want to grab her hips and drag my hand along her tight ass, but I can't. Not yet, so I settle with a long lingering look.

Big mistake because now my dick is hardening once again. If she turned around, she would see the tent pitching in my jeans.

Think of something not sexy. An old grandma with saggy tits. Tits. Annabell's tits are perfect. Fuck! Stop.

Well that didn't work.

Without hesitating I start unloading boxes from her car. She looks a little surprised as I give her a smile and head up stairs. Did she really think I wouldn't help her out? The workout will help my hard-on. Plus, I get to spend more time with her.

It only takes about fifteen minutes to bring all her boxes up. It's surprising how little she has.

"Thank you for the help. That was really nice of you, and not necessary at all," she says as she drops the last box down on the floor next to her bed. Her ass is on full display for me, and I can't help but check her out.

Damn that's a nice ass.

As soon as she turns back around, I drag my eyes up to hers, lingering on her boobs for a moment. She catches me checking her out, but I don't care. My tongue darts out to wet my lips. Imagining her bent over that bed with her ass in the air is all I can think about.

I need a cold shower.

Her eyes land on my chest. She scans me over, seeing my nipple piercings from under my t-shirt. Her eyes go wide. By her reaction, I'd say she is enjoying the view. She continues to roam over my body. I can feel her eyes on me. Every place she scans leaves a trail of heat.

As her eyes land on my thighs, I side my hands into my pockets. I'm doing everything in my power not to get hard as she watches me. Thankfully, I adjusted myself earlier so she shouldn't be able to see too much, but it is kind of hard to hide what she does to me.

Deciding to distract her, I grab the bottom of my t-shirt and pull it up to wipe some sweat off my forehead.

Yup, that did it.

Her eyes go wide as she quickly scans my abs. It's as if she is trying to take in the sight and memorize it before it's gone. I probably linger there for longer than I need to, but this is too delicious. Teasing her has become my new favorite thing.

"You okay, Ms. Annabell?" I continue my tease.

She doesn't snap her eyes to me like I thought she would. Instead, she slowly drags them up to my eyes over my chest as if it's a physical strain to remove her stare.

"Yes. I'm sorry," she finally says with a gulp. "I'm just thirsty from unpacking the car and bringing it up the stairs. It's hot outside. Is it hot in here? Are you hot? Or is it just me? Maybe we should turn the fan on." Her ramble is again the cutest thing I've ever heard.

"Oh, Ms. Annabell, it's not just you, I assure you that." I'm sweating so much right now, and it's not from the heat. It's from her. Reluctantly, I turn my back towards her. Immediately, I feel her eyes on me, checking me out as I once did her.

Flipping the fan on, I turn to her. "Maybe that will help cool you off for now. Let me know if you need help with anything. And I do mean anything." With that, I leave her alone with her thoughts.

A few hours later, after a long workout to rid my built up desire, I still can't stop thinking about her. The way her ass looked in her jeans when she bent over. The way her eyes widened when she was caught checking me out.

She was watching me like a starved animal. As if she hasn't eaten in days. I have plenty of food for her. She wanted to devour every last bit of me, and dammit I wanted her to.

I could see it in her eyes, and I loved every fucking minute of it. It took everything I had not to grab her and touch every inch of her so she never forgets my touch. I wanted to own her right there. I wanted to show her who I am.

But it's too soon. She isn't ready yet. She still needs time. I still need time to put everything into place. The first time I touch Ms. Annabell Brown will be the last time a new person touches her. She will be completely and utterly mine.

Chapter 15 Conrad

There is so much work I need to catch up on. After I left Annabell in her bedroom, I haven't seen her. I watched the camera in her room on and off. Knowing she is here gives me a sense of peace, but it's also driving me crazy.

I lay in bed unable to sleep. The knowledge that Annabell is just down the hall is killing me and preventing sleep. All I can think about is sneaking into her room and sliding into her bed with her. Then, slowly sliding inside of her.

I wonder what she would do? Would she fight me? Would she scream? Would she struggle? Would she give in once she realized it was me inside of her? Maybe she would pretend not to want it from her boss.

My phone interrupts my thoughts. The alert to Barbara's room goes off again.

Fuck. Not again.

I jump out of bed and pull on some sweatpants as fast as I can. I don't really feel like fighting an old woman naked.

Running down the stairs as quietly as possible, I make my way through the living room. Damnit, it's dark in here. I need to remember to turn a lamp on before I go to sleep.

As soon as I make it to Barb's room, I see she has managed to knock over the side lamp. She isn't awake enough to have to hold her down like I did the other day, so I quickly go to the locked cabinet and grab her medication.

I'm going to have to start giving her these medications more often apparently. Maybe she has a fast metabolism and can metabolize medications faster than most. Is that even a thing? I guess it would explain how she managed to stay so fit all these years.

Once I get her tucked back into bed, I clean up the glass as fast as I can. It's possible that Annabell heard that. I really don't want to have to explain why I'm cleaning up glass in a room where the resident is supposed to be comatose.

Exiting the room, I hear someone bumping into something. "Ouch!" I hear Annabell whisper.

Shit, I really don't want her down here right now. Just in case Barb's meds decide to stop working again. I mentally curse Zeak's guy for not being fast enough.

Waiting for her at the end of the hall, I grab her upper arm making her come to a halt. Without saying anything, I slid up behind her. I can feel her jump. Her breath begins to pick up. I'm having a hard time deciding if she is nervous that I'm touching her, or if she is scared. "What are you doing up, Ms. Annabell?"

"I'm sorry. I heard something and was worried. I wanted to make sure your mom was alright," she answers quietly.

Her back is against my bare chest as I hold onto her arm. I revel in the feeling before I say, "I told you, I don't need you until tomorrow. Now please, go back to your room."

I want nothing more than to keep her here with me in the dark. The things I could do to her in this pitch black hallway, but I can't have her out here right now.

She pulls out of my grip and stomps her way up the stairs. I can't help but laugh as she acts like a child being punished by her parents and made to go to their room.

She has no idea how much I want to punish her, but not in that way.

I had a hell of a time going back to sleep. After Annabell stomped off back to her room, I came to the office to watch her on the monitor for a few minutes. Once I saw her settling back in her bed, I got into mine only, I tossed and turned, thinking about the way her backside molded to my chest last night.

Dragging myself out of bed, I get my workout in early and shower. As the water runs down my naked body, I imagine Annabell with me. Only just down the hall, it's as if I can feel her when she is this close.

Unable to stop myself, my hand wraps around my already hard dick. I'm always hard these days, and it's starting to be a problem. I picture her in the shower in her room. She's slowly washing herself, her loofah working its way over her neck and down her arms. It slides down her flat stomach and between her legs.

Before I know it my come is spraying onto the shower wall. Even after I find my release, it's still not enough. It's not satisfying. I'm not sated. No matter how many times my hand gets me off thinking about her, it will never be good enough.

Frustrated, I dry off and get dressed for the day. Heading down stairs towards my office, I hear Annabell outside. Without thinking, I head to the side door. Just as I go to open it she bumps into me. Man, I sure do have perfect timing.

"Oh, I'm so sorry," she says in surprise. Looking up at me, she seems to be in a better mood than last night. Good. I wouldn't want to have to bend you over my knee and correct that attitude.

Who am I kidding? Of course I'd love nothing more than to do that, to feel that ass and see how wet it makes her.

She tries to side step me, but I don't move. I'm not ready to let her go. I want to make her squirm some more. She looks down nervously.

No, Princess. I want to see those beautiful eyes.

Placing my finder under her chin, I tilt her head up towards me. Her eyes lock with mine, and I can see the desire and mine match hers. Not wanting to push too hard too fast, I release her, turn, and walk towards my office.

Feeling her eyes burning into me like they were yesterday, I turn slightly and catch her. Her eyes go wide as if she is a deer in a spotlight. She has been caught and she wants to run, and so she does. I can't help but laugh as I walk into my office.

Taking a seat in my chair, I can't get the grin off my face. She is coming around very nicely.

Logging onto my computer, I switch to her bedroom camera. I log on just in time to see her walking towards the bathroom and turn on the shower. I had to stop myself from putting a camera in the bathroom. That may be crossing a line to watch her shower without her permission. I mean, even I have morals. Though they may be gray, they are still there.

As if her dog can sense me watching her, she starts barking. All I can do is thank that dog because when she barks, Annabell comes out of the bathroom naked. I'm leaning against my chair checking an email on my phone when I see her. Dropping my phone I pull the laptop as close to my face as possible. I feel like a teenage boy watching porn for the first time.

"Fuck me," I sigh.

It's only for a moment before she goes back into the bathroom, but it's enough to torture me more. I'm going to need another cold shower, possibly another workout.

Deciding I should do more work and less stalking for today, I log into my business network. We have had a few new investors for this month. While my assistant takes care of the paperwork, I'm left to shmooze them and see to it that they are being well taken care of.

After about an hour's worth of work, I check Annabell's cameras. I'm proud of myself for leaving her alone for a whole hour. When I click over to her bedroom, I see her looking herself over in the mirror.

Don't you know how beautiful you are.

She gives herself a onceover and heads out of her room. I guess it's time for me to tell her she won't be needed until next week. I wonder how she's going to take this?

I reach the kitchen just after she enters. She is looking the other way so she doesn't see me arrive.

"Good morning, Ms. Annabell," I say after I watch her for a few minutes. She jumps at the unexpected voice. She's so jumpy. This will be fun.

Before she speaks, she takes in the sight of me. I've changed into my slacks and white button down shirt for work. As she watches me, I walk towards her rolling up my sleeves to my elbows.

This is exactly what I'll do when I come home from work, but this work I'll enjoy immensely.

"Good morning, Sir. I mean Mr. Conrad," she says, slipping up. I internally growl. If I don't walk out of this kitchen right now, I'm going to pull her to her knees and make her call me Sir again.

"Turns out I don't need you to start working today. There are still a few kinks I need to work out. I will see you later, Ms. Annabell." I walk back into my office as quickly as possible.

As soon as I reach my office I shut the door, grab my laptop, suit jacket, and head to the office. Just being in the same space as her is making me crazy. I need some space.

"Franchesca, get Dallas Jackson on the phone for me," I call out to my assistant. He is one of the firm's top investors. We have both made each other lots of money, and I like to make sure he stays happy.

"Mr. Conrad, I have Dallas on the line for you."

"Thank you, Franchesca."

A second later I have Dallas in my ear.

"Lunch sounds like a fine idea Conrad."

"Perfect. I'll have my assistant call yours. We will set it up this week. I look forward to it," I say in my best "nice guy" voice.

"As always," Dallas replies.

It's not my favorite part of the job, but I enjoy all the food I've been blessed with experiencing. I always take my top investors to the best restaurants. Some I've even flown to New York and Colorado to thrill them.

I like the numbers, the puzzle side of it all. If I move this money here to invest it then this will grow so I can replace it over here. 2+2 doesn't always equal 4 in the investment world, and I love it.

Looking at the clock, it's about lunch time. I'm starving, and I need to check in on Annabell. Clicking over to the security camera, I watch Annabell unpack some of her boxes as she talks to her dog.

"Maybe I'll go to the store," I hear her say.

Wouldn't that be fun to watch her shop.
"Franchesca, I'm going out for lunch. Hold my calls. I'll be back when I can," I call out to her as I grab my keys and head out the door.

As I speed towards the mansion, I realize this would be much easier to install a tracker on her phone. On my way back, I spot her car on the road. Waiting for her to pass, I make a u-turn. What store are we going to today, Princess? I hope it has food.

I watch as she pulls into the small, local grocery store. She looks around, throwing random items into her basket. A few times she almost spots me. I need to sharpen up on my stalking skills.

There is something about watching someone when they don't know it. It's almost as if you get the real person that way. People act their true selves when they are alone and not trying to impress people.

After snacking on some beef jerky, I can't contain myself anymore. I walk up to her as she is trying to reach something on the top shelf. "Need some help?"

She stills mid reach. She knows it's me and her body is already reacting to me. Such a good Princess.

"Mr. Conrad, what are you doing here?" I see the shock on her face, and it makes me smile.

"Getting some duct tape. I ran out." I internally laugh. I can just imagine what she's thinking. *What do you need duct tape for, Mr. Conrad?*

"And what are you doing here, Ms. Annabell?" She tries to hide her basket from me. Little does she know, I've been watching every step she takes. Stepping closer, I hold onto the basket that dangles from her arm. Tampons, fruits, vegetables, condoms, and lube.

"Well, those definitely seem like essentials." I pull out the box of condoms. These will definitely come in handy, soon I hope. Without saying a word, I grin at her and place the box back in her basket.

"And this looks fun," I say as I pull out the lube. She covers her face from embarrassment.

Buckle up baby, you're about to be even more embarrassed. I step closer to her so she can hear me and on her. "But if he's doing it right, you won't need this." I place the lube back on the shelf because I don't plan on ever needing that with her unless she wants to try it, and in that case I'll try anything with her.

She starts to uncover her face. "I'll see you at home, Ms. Annabell."

I smile all the way back to my car as I open my second beef jerky and head back to the office.

Chapter 16 Annabell

I can't get him out of my head. No matter what I do, he is there. I can't decide if I want him renting space in my head or not. It's not an easy thing to deal with. On one hand, he is hot as hell. It's nice having eye candy. On the other hand, he is my boss. I can't get so distracted. Not to mention the never ending wetness between my legs.

I still cannot believe he caught me buying condoms and lube. Only…..he didn't let me buy it. Sure, I could have grabbed it off the shelf, but I left it there. *But if he's doing it right, you won't need this.* That was definitely flirting. I know I'm pretty crazy at times, but I'm not that crazy for that to just be in my head.

Does he never use lube? Maybe he never needs to. I'm sure every girl he touches simply drips for him. I know I have been, and he hasn't even touched me in my special places.

I can't help but laugh at myself. *Special places.*

The coincidence of him being at the grocery store the same time I was is impossible. Well I guess it's not completely impossible but it's pretty low chances just like me running into him on the sidewalk and then he happens to hire me. Or maybe I'm just finally entering into my good luck stage of life. I mean one can only hope right?

As soon as I got home from the grocery store, I decided to look around the mansion while Mr. Conrad was still out.

I've been dying to know what that locked door is in his garage. I mean what could he possibly be hiding in a padlocked door? I'm drawn to the garage, but I don't go in. The last thing I need is for him to come home and find me snooping in there again.

He doesn't seem like a very patient man to me, and I really want to keep my job. So, I decide to explore elsewhere.

I unfortunately don't get far when I hear a garage door open.

Crap. He's back.

Running up the stairs, I dive into my room. As soon as I open the door Haci greets me with her happy face. leaning against the door, I breathe heavily. Not from running up the stairs, but from being nervous from almost getting caught snooping. I mean, I guess this is my house now too. Don't I have a right to look around it?

Grabbing my bags, I start putting my clothes into the drawers and the closet. After hanging up and dispersing all of my clothes to their appropriate place, I start unpacking a few other items.

As soon as I open up the contents of what was once in my nightstand, I can't help but giggle. What I come face-to-face with is my very well used vibrator.

I can't help, but wonder if this trustee little sidekick will get as much action as it has in the past. Even when I was with Eric, he and I were still very acquainted.

Thoughts of Mr. Conrad helping me out in that department make my cheeks flush hot. I don't have to look into the mirror to know they are red.

Shaking my mind away from my dirty dirty thoughts, I stash the vibrator in my new nightstand. Just in case. You never know. But a girl can definitely hope.

After a couple of hours of unpacking and organizing my room, it finally looks like I live here. There was a gorgeous comforter already on the bed, but I swapped it out with my favorite one that my grandmother hand stitched for me. It's something I will always keep. I'm not sure what I'm going to do once it starts wearing thin.

Haci follows me everywhere I go, even to the closet. She still isn't quite sure what's going on, but I know she will get used to it.

As I'm laying on my new massively large bed reading, I get a craving for iced coffee. It's definitely a weakness of mine. It's one weakness I'm okay with. As I jump off the bed, I find myself wondering what other weaknesses I might stumble upon with my newly found boss.

Chapter 17 Conrad

I've been useless today. All I can think about is Annabell in the grocery store. Everytime I start to get some work done, I think about her. Thinking about her leads to me checking the cameras to see what she's doing. Then, that leads to me watching her for far too long. Then, my dick starts to get hard. I get frustrated, and start the whole process over.

What is wrong with me?

I've never acted like this before. I've never needed a woman so badly before. I don't know if I'll be able to take it for much longer. How long can I go? Watching my one day in and day out, not being able to touch her. It's torture, and I'm losing this battle.

Out of the corner of my eye, I see movement on the video in the kitchen. I see Annabell looking for something. Pushing away from my desk, I head for her. Trying to control myself when I see her bending over, I watch her.

"If I were coffee, where would I be?" She asks. Thinking she's alone in the kitchen, she continues to look for the coffee.

"Over to the right of the fridge." I say as I watch her spin around in surprise. Her eyes go wide when she sees me.

Surprise, Princess.

"Oh sorry, I didn't mean to disturb you. I was just craving some iced coffee." She almost sounds annoyed that I'm here. Someone needs an attitude adjustment, and I would love to be the one to give it to her.

Soon, Princess. Soon.

"Now, Ms. Annabell, you know you could never disturb me. I enjoy the interruption." She has no idea how much I am enjoying this interruption. I needed an excuse to leave my office and stop watching her on the computers. The real thing is so much better. My only issue now…I'm dying to touch her, and I don't think I can resist as I watch her reach for the coffee machine.

Without thinking, I glide my hand over hers. Big mistake. The feeling of her warm, soft hand has me dying to shove it into my pants. I want to feel her small hands wrapped around me. If she doesn't leave my side right now, I don't think I will be able to control myself.

Shit.

"I got this, Ms. Annabell. Go have a seat. I will bring it to you."

She's looking at me confused. Part of her looks as if she wants to eat me right up, but the other part looks as if she is frightened. I kind of like seeing the fear in her eyes, but seeing the lust in her eyes is even better. I must be a lucky man because I'm getting both at this moment.

Just as I'm about to turn and give my focus to the machine, her gaze drops to my lips, and holy fuck, she pulls her lips between her teeth. She's biting her fucking lip. How can I look away? How can I leave when she is looking at me with such desire.

Again, I can't help myself. I have to touch her. Even though I shouldn't because I'm not sure I can control myself around her. My hand is drawn to her lip like they are magnetized. I can't help it, but I don't really want to right now. I've wanted to touch those lips since I first saw her.

With my left hand still on the coffee cup, my right hand lifts to her face. It's seeking out her warmth because I know she is warm. I can see her cheeks heat up right in front of me.

Slipping my thumb along her bottom lip, I pull it out of her mouth. I'm tempted to slip my thumb into her mouth. I want to see her suck on it. I want to see what she would do with something inside of her mouth.

Her eyes drip with sex. She is so turned on I notice her breathing pick up. The movement makes my eyes drop to her chest. Her perfect tits rise and fall with her increased breaths.

All I want to do is take her in my arms and kiss her. I need to feel her against my body. I need her to feel my arms wrapped around her. I want her to know this is her place. She belongs in my arms.

She wants me to kiss her, and every fiber in my body is telling me to do it. But damn it, it's too soon. I can't scare her off. My brain is saying no, but I keep moving towards her. My hand drops to her waist because it belongs there. I belong here. She belongs here. I hover over her at first, but then I almost feel angry. I'm angry I can't have her yet. I'm pissed she is so close, and I can't have my way with her.

Fuck.

My hold on her tightens as my anger takes over. It tightens so much I see her eyes go wide with need. Her breathing is picking up, and mine mimics hers.

"Thank you, Sir. I'll go sit down now." She finally speaks as I find myself leaning closer to her. The only noise in this quiet kitchen were our deep breaths, so her words shock us both.

Reluctantly, I release her slowly. It's the last thing I want to do, but I bring my attention back to the coffee machine. Gripping the counter with both hands, I try to steady myself. I'm about to turn around and grab her. If I let go of this countertop, that's exactly what's going to happen. It's taking every ounce of restraint I have not to.

After several moments of deep breaths and thoughts of my grandma, I manage to make two amazing cups of iced coffee. Since I arrived at the mansion, I must say I've mastered this machine.

Setting down the glass in front of her, I watch as she examines the crystal glass I chose. It's a Dublin ice glass with a bendy straw. Without looking at me, she takes a sip.

"Wow, that is amazing!" She is surprised.

"I'm glad you like it," I say with a smile as I sit down next to her. Taking a drink of my own glass, I must agree with her. It is pretty freaking good.

I watch her as she drinks her coffee absentmindedly as if I'm not here. Is she still thinking about how close I was to her? If I had tried to kiss her, would she have let me? No, I don't think she would have let me. That's why I can't try anything yet. She needs to warm up to me. In her mind, I'm her boss. She's not going to risk this job for a guy. She doesn't know we are meant to be together yet, but she will.

As I watch her drink, I'm mesmerized by her movements with her straw. The way it moves in and out of her mouth. The way her tongue swirls around it. What I would give to be that straw though. I laugh as I realize I'm jealous of a damn straw. I laugh until I see her eyes find mine.

She raises her glass to her lips again, only this time she watches me as she plays with her staw. Her tongue licks at the tip of it. She sees the reaction I have, and she continues. Feeling my jaw tighten, I watch as she runs her tongue along the side of the straw.

Fuck! She needs to stop.

Grabbing my thigh, I hold on tight as I imagine her licking my dick that way. The heat in my eyes is evident. I know she sees because she turns her head and sets down the glass.

I see a smile start to form on her lips. She thinks it's funny to tease me like this? I'll remember that, Princess. You're going to wish you never did that.

"Thank you for the coffee. It really hit the spot." She goes to walk away, but I don't let her leave. She can't leave yet. Not until I plant the seed inside her head.

Grabbing her hand, I spin her around. Standing face to face, I say, "I can hit that spot much better, Ms. Annabell." The way her jaw drops is both priceless and tempting. Thoughts of her with that straw flood my mind. I could slip my finger inside her mouth so easily right now, or even my dick. I know she would do such a good job with it.

"Excuse me?" Her question comes out as almost a whisper. I shocked her. Good.

"You heard me," I say as I get off the stool and back her into the island. My hands go on either side of her, and I get so close to her my cheek is flush with hers. Her body stiffens. Is she scared this time? Or is she just so turned on she's having a hard time breathing?

I feel a smile come over me as I lean down to whisper in her ear. Being this close to her without being able to really touch her is causing me physical pain. I'm actually aching for her.

"Princess, I can hit every spot for you. All you have to do is ask." As soon as the words leave my lips, I visibly see her melt.

Did you like that, Princess?

I see her tongue dart out of her mouth causing me to follow the movement. I'm about to go too far. I'm about to cross that line. It's as if I'm watching myself from the sideline. I see it coming. I could stop myself, but I don't want to.

"I am absolutely a man that knows what he wants and takes it. But with you, I won't touch you unless you ask. When that day comes, you'll only have to ask once."

"Are you hungry?"

"God, so am I." I take a deep breath before I continue. "I'm so fucking hungry." I watch her as she processes my words. The way she is looking at me, I'd say she was just as hungry as I am.

Good.

"I'll order in for us. Go change and be back here in an hour. We will have an early dinner." I say. I'm not really asking her. This is what I want, so I sure as hell hope she does it. If not....part of me wants to tie her up and drag her down here.

I look over to the dining room chair. I can picture it now. Her, tied up in a seated position with her hands tied behind her back. Me, force feeding her something delicious like my dick. Just the thought has me growing hard. I better get her out of her before I make that daydream a reality.

She nods her head, and with shaky legs she starts to walk away when I back away from her. Watching her as she speed walks away, I can't help but smile. I'm going to have so much fun with her.

Sitting on my floor after getting in a quick workout, I haven't stopped thinking about how close I was to Annabell. I can't believe how much of a little minx she just was. She was teasing me. She was tempting me. It turned me on and pissed me off at the same time. She knew exactly what she was doing. Fuck, I wanted to be that straw in her mouth. I was in complete shock. The way her tongue rolled over it, she was begging for me to use her mouth.

I can tell she almost lost control. I was so close to just grabbing her and fucking her on that island regardless of the consciences. If she hadn't stopped, I would have. I would have shown her you don't need that 'for her pleasure' lube if you're doing it right, but she isn't ready for that.

Though it's going to be hard as hell to wait for her to ask me to touch her, I know she will. I know it will make the wait worth it. She will desire me. She will beg for me. I will make her wet and wanting. I will haunt her dreams and her nightmares. She will touch herself thinking of me. Her body will know my hands before I even touch her for the first time. She will be mine.

Chapter 18 Conrad

It's pathetic that I can't go an hour without jerking off. This woman is killing me, and she doesn't even know it. Although, maybe she does know it. But she isn't just any woman. She is my one. She's different. I haven't been myself since she arrived. You may think that's not a good thing, but it is. She makes me a better person. She's what I want.

As I let the water run down my body, I can't stop thinking about her in her room right now. She's probably in the shower right now, naked, thinking about me just like I'm thinking about her. She's probably running her hands over her body as she washes. I bet she's picturing me touching her. Maybe her hands are slipping between her legs as I stand here.

And now I'm stroking my dick thinking about her smooth lips being spread out by her shaking fingers. They shake as she's inserting a finger. They quiver as she rocks back and forth wishing it was my fingers on it. Rolling her hips because she can't take it anymore. Trying to get closer to what she wishes was me….and I'm exploding all over the shower wall.

What are you doing to me, Annabell?

Heading to my closet, I pick out a fitted white t-shirt. It's the most comfortable t-shirt I've ever owned, so I bought ten of them. They were ridiculously expensive, but I bought them with the old woman's cash. Sure, I have my own money, but it's fun spending hers. She doesn't deserve this blood money anyways.

Grabbing my lighter pair of relaxed jeans, I pair the outfit with my favorite white sneakers. I've always prided myself in my nice attire, but I did see the way she looked at me in my sweatpants.

Walking over to the trunk I have stored in the back of the closet, I pull out the scrunchie I have been carrying around with me. It lives in my pocket, but I think it's time to put it away. One day in the near future, I plan to be taking off my pants in front of Annabell. I don't want it falling out in front of her.

The trunk is full of keepsakes. I have several items from past women. It's not that I wanted those women to be my one, but it reminded me that one day I will find her. And now I have. I guess I could toss the items, but it's just a reminder of where I have come from.

The other items are a much darker keepsake. I've kept items from every person whose life I have ended. I know, it's very Dexter of me. It's probably not the smartest thing to do, but I've wiped them all clean and soaked them in bleach. There shouldn't be any trace of DNA on them.

Making my way downstairs, I see Annabell's room is still closed. Stopping in front of it, I lean my ear against the door. I hear her moving around. Her sweet voice sounds, and I'm pretty sure she is talking to herself.

Are you nervous, Princess? Good.

Tearing myself away from her door, I call in the food and head to my office. I could probably stand at her door and listen to her all day. Her voice is like butter and silk. Everytime I hear her speak, the hair on my body stands up. Even my hair stretches out to touch her.

Tempted to pull up the camera in her bedroom, I shut my laptop and work on organizing my desk. I hate when things aren't organized. It's probably one of my biggest pet peeves. Thankfully, Annabell seems very tidy. She's exactly how I like my girls…clean but dirty.

Looking at my watch, it's 3:05 and Annabell has not arrived yet. As soon as I got the text that the food had arrived, I came in and set everything up. I've been in the kitchen since 2:50. I thought she would be early. I thought she would be excited. I pictured her sitting at the dining room table waiting for me, ready. Though that could just be my imagination running wild.

I can feel my annoyance rise the later it gets. When I hear her coming down the stairs, it's 3:10. I'm leaning against the island with my arms crossed over my chest as I look at my watch. The moment she sees me she knows I'm aggravated.

"You're late," I huff. She jumps at my sudden words, and it excites me.

"I'm sorry," she sheepishly says as she plays with her fingers. She's nervous. As she should be.

Instead of speaking right away, I take this time to appreciate the view. She has picked out a shirt that hangs off her shoulder. My eyes linger on the exposed skin of her shoulder. What I would give to kiss that exposed skin. It's begging me right now. No, it's taunting me.

Letting my eyes fall down her body, I take my time and enjoy the sight. Her skin has flushed. Though, I'm not sure if it's because she is nervous or turned on. Honestly, it's probably both.

"Next time, be on time, Ms. Annabell." I turn to walk towards the dining room, but quickly realize she is not following me. "Follow me," I say over my shoulder. Thankfully, she does as she is told which makes me smile.

Reaching the dining room, I watch her reaction to the table. Laid out are two dinner plates with tops that cover them to keep the food warm, and beside the plates are our drinks. Water, a glass of red wine, and a glass of iced coffee. I decided to skip the straw this time. I don't think I could control myself watching her assault that straw again.

An amusing grin covers her face. "No straw this time?" She asks through a giggle.

"Not unless you want to be my dinner," I say without thinking.

Damnit.

The look on her face is worth the risk. She's shocked, but she is also excited. I don't think I will ever get tired of seeing her expressions change so quickly. She will go from nervous, to excited, to turned on, to scared all in the span of ten minutes. And I love it.

"I am pretty hungry, but I do like my straw. Do I have to pick one or the other?" Hearing her words, lights fire to my core, but I try not to let it show. Instead, I walk over to her chair and pull out the chair for her.

"Take a seat in the chair, Ms. Annabell, or I'd be more than happy to be your seat for the night." And there goes some more sexual innuendos. I just can't help myself.

"Yes, Sir," she says with a smirk, and as soon as those words brush past her lips I clench. My jaw tightens, and I have the sudden urge to grab her hair and pull her onto my lap. Screw this waiting game…but I resist.

I had set my plate across from her, but I think I need to be closer to her. Taking a seat next to her, I pull my plate and drink over in front of me. As I slide into my chair, I make an effort to graze her leg. It seems unintentional, but the fact that I don't move my leg says it all.

Feeling her stiffen at my touch has me craving more. I want to see just how much I can make her squirm.

"So, do you like Italian food?" I wait for her answer, but it doesn't come. Her fingers twist as her gaze lingers on our joined legs.

"Ms. Annabell?" She jumps at her name. She must have been deep in thought. I'm desperate to know what she was just thinking about.

"I'm sorry what?" Her soft eyes find mine.

"I said, I hope you like Italian. What were you thinking about?" I ask her point blank. I have a feeling she is going to resist, but I will get her to answer the question.

"I was just thinking about tonight's dinner."

Bullshit.

"What else were you thinking about? Just tell me. I want to know, Annabell," I say with the most serious and comforting voice I can muster up.

"I was thinking it was going to be a long dinner with your leg touching mine." Wow, she actually told me the truth. Part of me is wishing I didn't know she was thinking about my leg because all of me is thinking about what's between hers.

"Would you like me to move my leg?" I ask her as I stare down at her. She hasn't been able to make eye contact with me since I asked her.

"No!" She literally yells at me. I guess she really doesn't want me to move my leg. Good.

"What else were you thinking?" I ask, trying my hardest not to smile.

"What else?" I see that mind of hers running wild. She's so cute when she's nervous.

"Yes, what else were you thinking about, Ms. Annabell? There's no reason to be shy." She's thinking too much about this. I can't have her getting lost in her turmoil, so I lean in closer to her. The close proximity of her is torture. Looking down over her bare shoulder, I want to take a bite out of it. Instead, I say, "Tell me."

I stare her down until she speaks. "I was thinking about how it would feel to touch your leg. To feel every muscle in them," she finally admits.

"Fuck." The word slips from my lips before I can stop it. My gaze drops to my lap as I adjust myself. I can feel myself hardening thinking about her reaching over and touching my leg. She is a mantrap, and she doesn't even know it.

Pulling the lids off our plates, I say, "Eat! Our food is getting cold." I can't keep this up. She is going to kill me.

Stabbing at my food, I start devouring the delicious dish. Of course, thoughts of me devouring Annabell on this very table flood my mind.

The night I first found out where Annabell lived, I saw her making this. It didn't resonate with me at that moment. I was too busy getting off at the sight of her, but I'm glad I remembered it this afternoon.

Eating the rest of my food, I see her reach for her coffee. When I make eye contact with her, I see her smiling. She's thinking about that straw.

"Would you like a straw with that coffee?" I ask in a low voice.

"I would, actually, thank you." She smiles back at me with some attitude. And once again, I want to fuck that attitude out of her.

"Where are they?" She brings me out of my daydream.

"In the cabinet, left of the fridge, on the bottom right." I should just get up and get it for her. It would be a lot easier, but if I did. She most definitely would see my hard on.

"Where at? I don't see them?" Turning towards her, my jaw nearly breaks as I press my lips and teeth together. The shorts she has on have a huge rip on the ass cheek. I can see a good amount of her right ass cheek.

She's going to kill me.

"In the red metal basket," I say through gritted teeth. Damn this woman. She knows exactly what she's doing. She's toying with me. I've never liked the hard to get game, but for her, I'll play any game she wants.

She comes back to the table with a pep in her step. She's happy with herself. When she sits down, I make sure my leg isn't touching hers. I can tell she is disappointed. I think I've had all the teasing I can take.

"I'm sorry about last night. I didn't mean to wake you up and scare you," I finally say.

"That's okay. Was your mom alright?"

"Yes, she's fine. Just a little under the weather." Now I'd like for her to stop asking questions about Barbara. I don't necessarily enjoy lying to her.

"Do I need to see her?"

"You actually don't need to start until next week."

"Why?" Her attitude is back and roaring like a lion. She is definitely going to be fun to tame.

"She is under the weather, like I said. On Monday you will start seeing her,"

"You know, I am a nurse," she says with her cutest annoyed look, but she needs to stop.

"While I think your attitude is cute, it's not necessary. The reason I don't need you to start until Monday is because she is being seen by a medical doctor. Trust me, I'd love to see you work, but you will have to be patient, Ms. Annabell."

"Oh. I didn't realize. Well, I'm glad someone is seeing her." Glad that attitude is gone now, but I hate seeing the disappointment in her face.

"So where is your bedroom?" She pauses because I nearly choke on my wine. She wants to know where my bedroom is? I wasn't expecting that.

"I'm just asking so I know where to find you. I mean, if I needed to find you. I hope that's alright to ask. I'm not asking for any other reason." She rambles on. Biting her lip, I can tell she is trying to stop her rant. She doesn't even realize she is doing it, but that small act is driving me crazy.

I should be biting that lip.

"So you want to know where my bed is?" I ask her as I wink at her.

"What? No! I just wanted to know so I could know where to look for you," she stumbles over her words.

"You want to know where to look for me when I'm in my bed? Interesting." I set my glass down. Reaching up, I rub my chin as if I'm really thinking hard about this.

"Stop," she says through a laugh. And it's the most wonderful sound I've heard. "It would just be nice to know where to find you if I needed you."

"Oh, so now you need me? I told you all you had to do was ask, Ms. Annabell." She blushes at my words. She's picturing it.

"I do need you." She pauses and I about blow my load right there with the way she is looking at me. She twirls her hair as if she is innocent.

Oh, Princess. I already know.

"I need you to tell me where your bedroom is in case I need to find you in a purely platonic way, Mr. King."

Fuck.

The worst word I could hear right now. *Platonic.* My dick gets sad, and I get it. Seriously? There is nothing platonic here. She damn well knows that, but I'll play along for now.

"Sure, Ms. Annabell. If you need me, and I'm sure you will one day, I am upstairs just past your room at the end of the hall. Come see me anytime. Day or night." I put an emphasis on *night*.

"Where did your mind go?" I ask her when I see her eyes drift to the right.

"I was just thinking about how I should respond." She says with doe eyes. She looks as if she has been caught in headlights.

Good try, Princess.

"Bullshit," I abruptly say. We both know she is lying, and I don't like it.

"What? It's true."

"Now, Ms. Annabell, how can we work together if we can't trust each other? So tell me, where did your mind go?" I know she is going to give in. She might as well just give up the fight right now.

"You really want to know? I mean, are you sure?" She scrunches up her face. Does she really have to ask me that?

"Tell me."

She takes a deep breath. She's nervous to admit whatever it is she is about to say. "I was imagining myself coming to your bedroom door in the middle of the night, and you answer the door in nothing but boxer briefs." I can't hide my smile as she covers her face from embarrassment. Her cheeks are getting red, and my dick is growing with every passing second.

"Don't be embarrassed, Ms. Annabell. I like where your mind goes, but there is only one thing wrong with it," I say as she pulls her hands away from her face.

"What's that?" I give her my wicked smile because I can't help but toy with her. She is so enchanting when she is uncomfortable.

"Well, I sleep naked. So I'd be answering the door with nothing on." I pause for a moment and watch as the weight of what I just said sinks in.

"Oh boy." She lets out a deep breath. "Of course you do." The last part she said under her breath, but I still heard it which makes me smile even bigger. She doesn't see because her head is in her hands again.

"What do you sleep in?" I am so desperate to know, but I do my best not to let it show. I can see the hesitation in her eyes. Why does she do this? She knows she's going to give in to me.

"Just tell me. We both know you're going to answer my questions."

With a deep sigh, she does as she's told. "I usually sleep in an oversized t-shirt and my underwear."

Fuck me.

The visual of her in my t-shirt, with her panties barely visible has my dick aching. I'm not sure I can take much more of this, but I continue torturing myself.

"No bra?" She doesn't hesitate this time. She's learning.

"Definitely not. I don't even want to wear one right now."

Fuuuuuck!

Is she serious right now? Is she trying to make me explode inside of my pants? Does she know what she is doing to me? Or is she just naturally alluring?

"By all means, make yourself comfortable. It is your home too." Every cell in my body is begging her to rip her bra off and beg me to touch her, but she doesn't

"I think I'm getting a little too comfortable with my boss as it is," she pouts.

No, this is not the direction I wanted this conversation to go, damnit.

"Not possible," I try to reassure her. This is what I want. I want you, and you know it.

"Do you mind if I ask what happened to your mom?" And she changed the conversation. I need to bail.

"I don't mind you asking, but I think that's all for tonight. I have to get some work done."

"But it's only just past five o'clock," she says with a pout. Those pouty lips are going to look so good wrapped around my dick. Just you wait.

"Yes, get some rest, Princess. I'll see you tomorrow." I start to walk off towards my office, but then I remember something.

"Oh, and Ms. Annabell, don't ever wear those shorts around me again unless you want me to rip them off of you. And trust me, I will take that as an invitation. Have a nice night." I walk off with a smile. Secretly, I hope she wears them again. I would love an excuse to rip them off of her.

Chapter 19 Conrad

Sitting in my office, I see that it's almost 2am. I'm shocked. Sure, I always work late but never past midnight. Closing my laptop, I grab my phone and head upstairs. Feeling my phone buzz, I look to see who the hell is texting me this late.

Rachel: Can I come over?

I haven't heard from Rachel in a few days. I thought I had finally gotten through to her that this was over. I had someone keep tabs on her for a while. She settled into her new position I helped her get. Other than the occasional text, she seemed to have accepted it and moved on.

Conrad: No. Go to sleep.

Rachel: I love it when you tell me what to do.

She sends me a picture of her in nothing but some lace panties. Normally, I'd be telling her to get over here so I could put my dick inside her and send her on her way, but I have no desire to. The only person I want my dick in is Anne, and I want it inside of her more than I have ever wanted anything.

Conrad: Then do what you're told.

Rachel: Why can't I come over? Have you met someone else? Is that what this is about? I thought things were going well with us.

I really don't want to have this conversation again.

Conrad: We have been over this, Rachel. I know you're just drunk. Turn your phone off and go to sleep.

Rachel: ☹ Yes, Sir.

I'm not sure what is with her submissive side tonight, but I can't help but imagine Annabell on her knees saying that.

Thankfully, Rachel doesn't text me again. I'm sure she has passed out by now. Hopefully she doesn't remember texting me and won't bother me again. I'd really rather not deal with her anymore. I'd hate for Annabell to notice her texting me one day. That's just what I need.

Making my way to my closet, I pull off my shirt and toss it into the hamper. Knowing I need to get some sleep I make my way to turn off my light, but my phone buzzes again.

I'm ready to press ignore thinking it's Rachel, but it's not. It's Zeak.

"It's about damn time," I say as I answer.

"Sorry, boss. It's been taking longer than I expected," Zeak whines into the phone. I would consider Zeak to be a friend. Probably my only friend. I've never been able to make friends easily. Even in school, I was a loner. At the time I hated it, but it made me who I am today…very independent and successful.

"I need it by Sunday night," I say, but I try not to get too upset.

"I'll do my best. If I could go get it myself, I would. But I don't know where they are. My contact won't tell me. He keeps giving me the run around, but he says they will be here soon."

"Do your job or I'll find someone else to do it." I'm not so nice this time. Zeak knows it's not personal. It's just how I do business. I don't like not getting my way, and it shows.

"I'm handling it, boss. I'll get it to you by Sunday," Zeak promises.

"Good. Get it done." I hang up the phone just as I see movement out of the corner of my eye. Walking toward my door, I see the sexiest little snoop running back to her room.

I want to grab her by the hair, pull her back to my bedroom, and show her how I handle snoops. I don't though. I simply smile and watch as she ducks back into her room. She wanted to see me. She wanted to know what I was doing. She's curious about me. Good. I know I didn't say anything to incriminate myself, but I'll have to be more careful now that I know my girl likes to sneak around.

Smiling, I turn off the lights and crawl into bed. I decided to leave my door open, just in case I have any snoopers that would like to watch me sleep. I can't help but hope she does. With the storm lulling me to bed, I fall asleep dreaming of her crawling into my arms.

Waking up with a smile still on my face, it quickly fades when I see what time it is. It's 9 am. I can't remember the last time I slept this late. Usually my body wakes me up at 7 am at the latest. I've always had a natural alarm clock.

Pulling on my sweatpants, I quickly look around the mansion for Annabell. She isn't in her room. I don't see her in the kitchen or living room. Heading to my office, I pull up the cameras. She is nowhere to be found.

Where the fuck are you, Princess?

Panic overtakes me. I run up to her room, and unlock her door. Of course I have a key. Sure, I said she was the only one that had one, but obviously I mean she was the only one other than me.

Her dog barks at me for a moment. "Hey girl. Can't we be friends?" I hold out my hand to her. Thankfully, she sniffs it and starts to wag her tail. "See, I knew you would start to like me eventually. I'm not mad at you for barking at me. You're just protecting your mom, and I'm grateful for that. But I'm here now. I will protect both of you." Giving her dog a quick pet on the ears, I continue my search.

"Annabell, are you in here?" There is no answer. I don't really expect there to be one, but I was hoping.

"Where did your mama go?" I ask her dog. "If only you could speak." She wags her tail once again.

Taking the opportunity, I look around her room. Running my fingers along her dresser, I grab her hairbrush. Touching the strands of hair that remain, I picture pulling strands of her hair out of her while I fuck her. Returning it to its exact place, I move on to the bed.

Sliding into the bed, my dick instantly gets hard when I smell her pillow. It smells just like her. It's torture and arousing at the same him. Crossing my ankles and placing my arm behind my head, I picture her riding me like this.

I'm going to fuck you in this bed soon, Princess.

Getting out of the bed before I pull out my dick and ruin her sheets, I make my way to her closet. Gliding my fingers over her clothes, I find myself getting excited to see her in each and every one of these outfits.

Unable to help myself, I look through her underwear drawer. I'm so tempted to take a pair, but I want them to smell like her pussy. Looking around for her dirty clothes hamper, I spot it on the left of her built-in drawers. Finding what I'm looking for, I pull the used underwear to my nose and sniff in a deep breath. Letting out a huge desired filled moan, my dick pushes against my jeans.

You're going to have to wait until later buddy.

Sticking the gray painties into my pocket, I head to leave. "Remind me to put a tracker on your moms phone, okay," I say as I kneel down to her dog. "I have to go find her. You stay here," I say as I close and lock the door.

Oh where are you, Annabell?

Running down the stairs, I look for her car outside. Gone. Running back to my office, I pull up the outside cameras to see when she left. Rewinding the feed, I stop when I spot her outside around seven this morning.

You left that early?

Letting out a sign of relief when she goes back inside, I fast forward until I see her exiting the house. Only fifteen minutes later do I see Annabell getting into her car. Tension rises in my shoulders. I don't like that she left without me knowing. I don't like that I don't know where she is or who she is with.

She better not be with a guy. I will end him.

Engrossed in my search for Annabell, I jump when I hear my phone ring. Zeaks name flashes on my screen.

"You better be calling me with good news."

"Always," he replies smugly.

"So that means you have the medicine?" He better not be messing with me. I am not in the mood.

"I do. Want me to drop it off?" I think for a moment. I really won't want Annabell to come home and find some random guy here. I'd have to explain, and I hate lying to her, even if it's necessary.

"Can you be here within the next thirty minutes?" Surely she won't be back that soon, but if she does. I'll just say he is an employee. That's the truth.

"I'll be there in twenty," he says just before he hangs up. And that's exactly why Zeak is the best.

Making my way into the kitchen, I scramble some eggs. I don't feel very hungry, but I know I need to eat if I want to get my workout in. Just as I'm turning off the burner, I hear the doorbell.

Looking at my watch I'm surprised. It's only been ten minutes. I guess Zeak is even better than I thought.

Opening the door without looking through the peephole, I curse myself.

Always check the peephole, Conrad. Rookie mistake.

Instead of Zeaks dark skinned face, I see a dark haired girl that once excited me. "Rachel, what are you doing here?" Forget about having to explain Zeak to Annabell, how would I explain Rachel to her? I can't imagine that would go over too well. We're not at the point in our relationship where Annabell would fight for me. This would probably push her away, and I can't have that.

"I wanted to see you and you were ignoring my calls," Rachel pouts. Did she call? I didn't even realize. I was too busy worrying about where my girl is.

"I didn't know you called. Plus, it's only nine in the morning. What do you want?" I ask as coldly as possible.

"I want you to give me a second chance," Rachel says as she steps closer to me.

"I already hired someone else, Rachel," I say ignoring her actual meaning. I know she isn't talking about work.

"Screw her, I don't care about the job. I want a second chance with you. I can't get you out of my head. I'm sure your head has been thinking about me," she says as she drops her gaze to my dick.

Normally this sexual tease would do it for me. I'd have her naked in five seconds, but it's not working on me anymore. All my head wants is Annabell, but I can't tell her that. I know if I do, it will make things even worse.

"So you just want to fuck?" I ask. I want to see what she will say to that. If I can make her think it was just about the sex, maybe she will get over this.

"I would love to get on my knees and suck your big cock." She licks her lips and drops to her knees. Again, normally this would have me hard as a rock, but I got nothing. Really, I'm kind of annoyed. I'm going to be pissed if Annabell sees her.

"Get up, Rachel. We aren't going to fuck. It's not going to happen." For once, I'm at a loss for words. Part of me wants to tell her I've moved on, but I don't want her asking with who.

I pull her up off of her knees. She really isn't getting the hint. As soon as she is on her feet, her lips meet mine. This is bad. I have to get this girl away from me...away from this house, but before I can. Someone interrupts us.

"Is this the new girl?" I hear Zeak ask.

Fucking shit. Are you kidding me right now?

Before I can say anything, Rachel barks out, "New girl? Is that why you don't want to be with me anymore? You found someone else?" I give Zeak a death stare.

I'll deal with you later.

He gives me an apologetic look. Yeah, that's not going to help me right now. "No, he meant you. I just haven't had a chance to tell him we parted ways." She places her hand on her hip and gives me a pouty face.

I lie through my teeth because if I don't, she will know about Annabell. I really don't want her anywhere near her. Zeak knows about Annabell, but he doesn't know the whole story. Thankfully, he isn't one to ask.

"Who is this?" Rachel asks. I'm thankful to answer. I'm glad for the subject change.

"This is Zeak. He is my associate. We have some business to take care of. Have a nice day, Rachel." That's my polite way of telling her to *get the fuck off my property.* Even though it's not technically my property.

"This isn't over," she says as she walks back to her car.

Oh but it really is.

I don't justify it with a response. I simply give her a two finger wave.

"Who the hell was that?" Zeak asks as he walks into the mansion.

"My crazy ex. She won't leave it be," I admit to him.

"Want me to take care of her?" Zeak isn't a hit man, but I know he would do it if I asked him to.

"No, she won't be a problem. Let's go to my office."

I didn't know it at the time, but I would come to regret not taking Zeaks offer.

Chapter 20 Conrad

Once Zeak left the house, I gave Barbara her new medicine. Already, her vitals seem more stable. Good. Now Annabell can safely start working come Monday.

Annabell has been gone for over four hours. The longer she is gone, the more pissed off I get. My anger is turning to concern as the minutes go by. This will never happen again. She will never be able to go somewhere without me knowing.

Heading to my makeshift gym, I get in my workout. Overdoing it, I try to pump out the worry through the weights. If she is gone much longer, I'm going to get Zeak to find her.

Once I shower and eat my lunch, I send a text to my cleaning lady.

Conrad: I left dirty dishes in the sink, sorry.

Rosita: Mr. King, there is no need to apologize. That is what I'm here for.

Conrad: You're the best.

Rosita: I know.

I have had Rosita with me since I moved into the mansion a few months ago. I hate leaving a mess for her to clean up, but I know that's her job. I've always been a clean freak, but I just don't feel like washing dishes today.

Back in my office, I watch the cameras as I catch up on work. Out of the corner of my eye, I see a car pull up. It's not Annabell's car, but to my surprise, she gets out of it. She stumbles a little as she turns around to talk to whoever is in the car with her.

Is she drunk?
Who the fuck is she with?

I zoom in to see, but it's unclear. Pushing off, I quickly head to the living room. I want to make sure she sees me before she goes to her room.

Hearing her open and shut the door, I don't hear anything else. Taking a step closer to the hall, she runs right into me. Her head thuds against my chest. I wasn't expecting her to be running…. but lucky me.

"We are making a habit of running into each other like this, Princess. At least it wasn't as bad as the first time though," I say as I watch the realization flood her mind.

Of course I remember the first time we ran into each other.

I reach out and steady her, but drop my arms quickly. I want so badly to touch her, but I said I would wait until she asked me to. What a stupid thing to say.

"Oh, Mr. Conrad. I'm so sorry." Her right hand comes up to my chest where she headbutted me. It lingers there for longer than it needs to, but hell if I'm going to stop her. To my delight, she starts to explore my chest.

With every movement, my chest tightens. When she grazes my pecs, my muscles tense. When both of her arms come up to inspect my shoulders, I have to pull my hands into fists to keep from touching her. Her hands smooth down the length of my arms, feeling the strength in them.

Yes, Princess. They will one day be wrapped around you.

Her hands glide down to my abs, and I nearly lose all control when her fingers tease the top of my jeans. Her eyes go wide when she looks down and sees my hard dick trying to escape.

That's all for you.

And then…. She dips her finger tips into my jeans, and I suck in air. It's the only thing I can do right now.

Fuck. Stay in control.

I want her to continue. I want her to unzip my jeans, and end my suffering. I want her to pull my dick free and give it the much needed attention it's desperate for.

Her eyes lock on mine, and she almost seems scared. I feel the fire in my eyes. I feel the desire dying down though. I know she sees it too. I know she feels it too. I wonder how wet she is right now? I'm desperate to feel her…to bury my face between her legs and finally taste the arousal I've been dying to try.

Seeing her eyes flick down to my impossibly harder dick, she bites her lip.

"Are you just going to stare at my dick or did you want to do something with it?"

Her eyes snap up to mine once again. She doesn't answer, but I can see it playing in her eyes like a film. She is picturing me being inside of her.

Soon.

Circling her, I study her as if she is my prey. I can't help but smile when I see she is wearing the shorts I warned her not to wear. "Bend over, Princess."

She doesn't listen right away. I can tell she is processing. The alcohol is altering her mind which might bode well for me. "I will not repeat myself," I growl into her ear. She jumps in response which makes me smile.

Doing as she's told, she bends over. Getting an amazing view of her luscious ass, I lick my lips. My hands are itching to touch her. "Do you remember what I said about these shorts, Princess?"

I wait for my response, but it doesn't come. She needs a good smack on the ass. "Is this my invitation?"

"Stand up," I say, unwilling to wait any longer. Pressing my chest against her back, I revel in the feel of her ass against my dick. "Take them off," I order her, whispering in her ear.

"What?" I guess she isn't speechless after all.

"Ah, I see you found your voice." I give her a half-smile. "I don't like repeating myself, Princess." Slowly, she unbuttons her shorts and lets them fall to the ground. I watch her from behind as she steps out of them and kicks them in front of her.

Admiring her black lace panties, I can't help but rub my dick on the outside of my jeans. I'm begging for a release. I'm not one to beg, but I would for her. I would get on my hands and knees for this girl.

"Bend over, Princess," I growl as I continue to rub my throbbing dick. Surprisingly, she does what she is told right away.

"Fuck, you look good enough to eat. Which I will do one day." I cannot wait for that day. I order her to stand back up as I circle her once more.

Face to face with her, my curiosity gets the best of me. "I'm curious about something, Princess." I pause for a moment, watching her reaction. My eyes drop down to her heaving chest. She is just as turned on as I am. "Does your bra match?"

I see her mouth open, but before she can answer, I interrupt her. "On second thought, how about you take that shirt off and just show me?"

She seems to have finally mustered up some courage because she doesn't miss a beat. "Yes, Sir." Those two little words speak straight to my dick. She smirks knowing the effect it has on me.

"You know, Princess. I did not like not knowing where you were today. That can't happen again. You will give me your number as soon as you go change," I say as I step closer to her. She is going to know just how much I did not like her being gone today.

"Yes, Sir," she says without missing a beat.

Such a fast learner.

"If you don't want me to rip those panties off of you, beat that ass red, and pound it until you're screaming, I'd get yourself upstairs right now." I'm going to be going to take a cold shower after this, and jerking off like I'm in middle school.

I don't take my eyes off of her. As she slowly walks up the stairs, I watch as she turns back around. "I'm going to go take a bath."

Fuck. Why is she torturing me?

"Is that an invitation to watch?" God, I hope that's an invitation. Though, it's just going to tease me even more.

"Okay," she says shyly.

"Just okay? I need more than that, Princess."

"That would be pretty hot if you watched me. Though, I'm not going to lie, that will make me super nervous," she bites her lip and tilts her head.

Running up the few steps she managed to take, I stand so close to her I can feel the heat coming from her body. "I like you being nervous."

"I will look. Shit, I won't be able to take my eyes off of you, but I won't touch you. I won't touch you until you ask, Princess. I've told you that. No matter how badly I want to rip these undergarments off you. Now get up there before I break my promise."

She runs so fast up the stairs, you'd think I was chasing her. The thought of chasing her upstairs making her fear me when I catch her, has me quite literally drooling over her bouncing ass.

When I enter her room, she has already started the bath water. Man am I glad Barbara decided to put a random ass bathtub in the middle of a guest bedroom. What she was thinking when she built this room, hell if I know. I only know I'm thankful as fuck she did.

She runs into the bathroom once the tub is filled. She still hasn't looked at me. She's too nervous. I hope she doesn't lose her nerve. I really want to watch her bath. As she's in the bathroom, I make myself comfortable on her bed. I'm propped up against her headboard when she emerges with only her robe on.

How am I going to keep from touching her?

Her eyes connect with mine as my hand rests lazily over my agonizingly hard dick.

"I like your eyes on me, but I want you to get in that hot tub and let me watch you, Princess." She steps into the water, still having her robe on. She slowly takes it off in a way that doesn't allow me the pleasure of seeing her naked body.

Damnit.

It's even more torturous not being able to see her body. Although, I'm not sure what I'd do if I saw her bare pussy right now. Sinking into the tub, she lets out a beautiful moan.

"You know, I can make you moan louder than that without even touching you."

"How is that, Mr. Conrad?" She's feeling brave. Well, let's see how brave you are Ms. Annabell.

"Touch yourself," I demand. She seems shocked by my order

"What do you mean?" Is she really confused about what I said? Or is she just trying to buy time to work up the courage? Either way, I make sure to be very clear so there is no question about what I want.

"Take your fingers, slide them between your legs, and rub yourself." She takes a deep breath. There is movement under the water, so I assume she did as she was told.

"Close your eyes and imagine those fingers rubbing on you are mine." She lets out a moan, and I have to remind myself not to move off of this bed.

"That's it. Now keep your eyes closed." I pull out my dick and slowly start moving up and down. Just the little friction is giving me satisfaction. God, how I wish it was her hand on me.

"Grab your tit with your other hand," I growl. My desire is starting to take over. I don't speak for a while. I just enjoy the sight of her as I rub my dick, but when she opens her eyes, I can't help but smile.

"Fuck," I hear her whimper. She has just caught me rubbing my dick to the sight of her. With her eyes on me, I start pumping faster. My left hand is still behind my head, propping me up to give me a great view of her. My legs have fallen open, giving her a great view of my length.

She bites her lips as she watches me continue my assault on myself. Rolling my finger against the tip, I imagine it's her tongue. She is so consumed in what I'm doing, she forgets what she is doing.

"Why did you stop?" I ask her, freezing in my position.

"I-I-I don't know," she stumbles her words out.

"I didn't tell you to stop, Princess," I say as I get off of the bed. Reluctantly, I tuck myself back into my jeans. Leaving them undone, I make my way over towards her. She visibly pouts when I put my dick away.

You like that don't you? Good. But you're going to have to work for it.

I watch her as she watches me stalk over to her. Like a lion walking up to his prey. She's a poor gazelle, trapped in the bathtub, but don't worry. I won't catch you yet. I love to play with my food.

"Why did you stop?" I ask as I walk up beside the tub. She is scanning my body. Her eyes haven't settled on one place for too long. She doesn't respond, so I assume she is too lost in thought to have heard me.

"Annabell." She jumps at the sound of her name.

"I'm sorry, what?" Taking in a frustrated breath, I look down at her. "You know I don't like repeating myself, but I'll do it once for you. I did not tell you to stop. So, why did you?"

"I couldn't help it," she whispers as she looks up at me. She is utterly breathtaking like this. Her cheeks are pink from her arousal. Her lips have been slightly parted since she got into the bathtub, making me want to slide my length between those puffy lips.

"I need more," I growl. I'm horny as fuck, and if she doesn't start telling me what I want to hear I may lose my patience.

"I was distracted by you. I mean, how could I not be?" She finally admits.

Good. I want that.

I love the effect I have on her. It makes me think things could quickly progress for us. "You want to watch me?" My breath is starting to pick up as I watch her nod her head.

"Tell me what you want to see, Princess."

"I want to see what your body looks like," she childishly says. Is she embarrassed to admit that she wants to see my body? But I know that's not it. I know she wants more.

"What else?" I demand. She needs to stop being coy and just tell me what she wants. She bites her bottom lip.

On instinct, the sight causes me to reach out to her, but I stop myself before I touch her. She pouts when I pull my hand away.

Princess, why won't you just ask me to touch you?

"I want to see you get off while watching me." She finally answers, and when she does, I almost lose myself. All of my self control I've been holding onto almost goes out the window.

"Fuck." The word slips through my gritted teeth. Knowing she wants to watch me has my dick begging to come back out. My head instinctively falls back, and I want nothing more than to give her what I want.

"Continue, Princess. If you want me to give you what you want, you need to give me what I want," I growl as I start to pull myself out of my jeans. It actually hurts to pull my dick out. I need to cum before I get blue balls, and I have a feeling I'll have a recurring issue with this girl.

As soon as my dick comes eye level to her, she licks her lips. My balls tighten at the thought of releasing into her mouth.

Fuck.

I want her. I want all of her. I want her mouth. I want her pussy. I want her hands. I want her ass. I want everything when it comes to her. I want to fill all of her holes, possibly all at once. The thought excites me.

Will she let me?

Her movement under the water starts to drift off. She hasn't taken her eyes off of my dick. "If you stop, then I'll stop," I remind her.

I can see her body start to tighten. She is getting close, and I want to see her cum as I watch her.

"Shove a finger inside of you. Don't take your eyes off of me," I pant as I continue stroking myself.

"Think about my fingers inside of your pussy. I want to grab your tits right now. They look so fucking tasty. Touch them again for me. I want to watch your nipples pucker up."

My pumps are getting faster and faster. It's not going to take much longer for me, and my little Princess is coming apart right before my eyes. Then, she raises out of the water enough for me to see her hard nipples.

Damn it.

This is the first time seeing her pebbled peaks, and I'm consumed by them. The way she rolls her left nipple…it's mesmerizing. The way her body is tightening and lifting out of the tub, I know it's time.

"That's it, Princess. Cum for me," I purr as I'm about to reach my own orgasm. I tell her to cum, and she cums. Her whole body shakes in beautiful spasms. Her release takes over her body in waves, and she rides them like the tide.

Tilting my head back, I explode into the bathtub. Pumping myself dry, I let the ecstasy flood over me. Meeting her eyes, she is sated and happy. Her head is spinning a little from the exhaustion. She needs to sleep.

Looking down at the tub, I smile. With the thought of her soaking in my cum, it starts to make me hard again. Watching her cum for me was life changing. If I wasn't already hers…I would be now.

Chapter 21 Annabell

My eyes close as my orgasm rolls through me. My head spins as I forget where I'm at. Opening them just in time to see Mr. Conrad shooting his cum right into the bathtub I'm in. I'm shocked. It's dirty. It's raw, and It's hot as hell.

Watching him as his eyes roll back into his head is probably the sexiest thing I've ever seen in my short life. Pair it with the growling sound he just made when he got off, I'm lost. I watch him. That's all I've been able to do. Waiting for my next instructions, I keep watching him. I keep waiting. I'm basically a lost puppy at this very moment.

His eyes meet mine. The fire that was once there has started to fade out. It's replaced with sorrow.

Why are you sad Mr. Conrad?

Is he disappointed? Does he regret this? I sure hope not because that will make for one awkward work life. Hell, since I live here it will just be an awkward life. Period.

"Stand up," he orders. He grabs my robe that is pooled on the ground. Holding it up at eye level, I stand up.

Since the robe is held so high, he can't see anything lower than my face.

Does he not want to take a peek?

I wouldn't even be mad if he did. After what we just did… I think we have already crossed that line. I clearly got to see him, and holy hell it was a beautiful sight. Sliding my arms into the robe, I step out of the tub. I'm soaked, so the robe clings to me.

Stepping out of the tub, my feet dig into the fluffy bath mat. I'm nervous to look up at him. I'm feeling incredibly shy with his close proximity.

So many thoughts run through my mind: What will happen next? Will he kiss me?

God, I want his lips on mine.

Will he take me to bed? Will he make love to me? Conrad King doesn't seem like the kind of man to make love. I take him for a man that solely fucks, and I'm sure he does it hard. I'm sure it's full of never ending pleasure. I'm sure he does it so well he makes every woman's toes curl. I would be okay with that… I think.

"Have a good night, Annabell," he whispers to me as he searches my eyes. Then, he turns and walks out of my room before I can respond.

What the hell?

Feeling rejected, pissed off, and happy all at the same time, I go to get dressed. Picking the most comfy, non-sexy clothes I own, I grab a bag of chips I brought over from my old apartment. I sure hope they are still good, but I'm eating them anyway.

Jumping up on my bed, I snuggle in and power on my laptop. I might as well get comfortable because there is no way in hell I'm leaving this room.

Feeling warm hands cover my body, I smile. The covers are pulled tight around me forming a cocoon. It's warm under here. It's safe. It's even comforting. I'd love to stay here forever.

Waking with yet another thunderstorm, I look down at myself. Was I just dreaming? I see I'm tucked into bed. The laptop that was once on my bed is gone. The chips I was eating are neatly placed on the bedside table with a chip-clip I know I didn't put there.

How did that happen? Who did that?

Maybe I did it while I was half asleep so I don't remember. Maybe it was Mr. Conrad. Could it have been him? Did I leave the door unlocked? If it was him…was that sweet or creepy? Sweet because he was trying to take care of me. Creepy because he snuck into my bedroom. Why can I not help but think it was sweet?

Chapter 22 Conrad

For the past day I have been avoiding Annabell. I know it's a dick move, but now that I've seen her in that way, I'm worried I won't be able to control myself. I need to see the rest of her. I wanted to peek at her body so badly when I held the robe up for her, but I didn't. She probably thought I was being a gentleman, but I wasn't. I was trying to keep myself at bay.

To be honest.... I was regretful. Not for what we did, but for what we didn't do. I know she still needs time, but I feel empty without her. I've never felt that way before. I've never waited for a woman before, and dammit it's the worst.

She is all I've thought about. She has invaded my days, my nights, and my dreams. I can't get any work done. I've been working out non-stop. I've been jerking off in the shower like a crazed sex addict. That's what I've become in the last 24 hours all because of one girl.

Hello, my name is Conrad, and I'm a sex addict.

It would be funny, but it's completely true. This morning, I sent an email to Franchesca telling her to get the documents off of my desk and scan them to me. Only I didn't say desk. I said dick. I told my very attractive assistant to grab papers off my dick.

Thankfully, she reacted professionally. She simply asked me to clarify. After apologizing profusely, she got me what I needed. She said it was no big deal, but I pray to God it doesn't change our work relationship. That's just what I need right now, having to find a new assistant because the last one is now filing sexual harassment charges aginst me. How would I explain that to Annabell?

I still can't believe Annabell wore those shorts again after I told her not to. I promised I wouldn't touch her until she asked, but dammit I wanted to fuck her so bad. I wanted to pull those shorts off of her the moment I saw them and sink my dick inside her.

Thankfully, she was a little tipsy when she came home, and I was able to take advantage of that. But who the fuck was she with? She won't be leaving this house again without me knowing where she is going and who she is with. That's not how this is going to work.

Of course, I was too damn distracted to get her phone number. Obviously, Zeak got it for me days ago, but I can't just start texting her. What would I say? *Oh I had my hacker find your phone number for me. It was pretty easy. Thanks for asking.* I haven't been able to install the tracker on it yet. That's next on my to do list.

The first thing on my to do list is…. STOP THINKING ABOUT HER IN THE BATHTUB.

Watching her come apart was like finally taking a breath of fresh air out of the water. It was everything, and I need more. I've been breathing underwater for far too long; I never even realized it until I found her. Who knew one girl could change my entire world? I haven't even really touched her yet, and I am putty in her hands. She just doesn't know it.

She's all I think about. She has become my obsession. One thing I do know, I will never let her go. I will never be without her, no matter what. She will be mine. I will make her mine any way possible, and I won't apologize for it.

I spent most of yesterday in the office playing catch up. People have been asking where I am. I want to tell them to all mind their own damn business because I'm the boss. I can do as I please, but it's probably not the best look for the company. I still need to play my role.

I need to keep busy. I've been getting that familiar itch. The itch to seek out one of those evil monsters that prey on the innocent and weak. My skin has been begging for me to let it feel the blood dripping from my hands.

Not just anyone will do, it has to be someone that is corrupted. Someone that hurts the innocent. I haven't even had time to go looking. I've been completely consumed with all things Annabell, but I guess that's what I wanted.

Thinking of Annabell, I pull up the cameras in her room. I see her bed is empty. It wasn't empty last night when I tucked her into bed. The poor thing fell asleep with a half eaten bag of chips at her side.

Placing the chips and laptop onto the bedside stand, I allow myself to touch her soft skin. She is asleep, it won't hurt. Her skin is warm under my fingers. Goosebumps pucker her skin as I continue down her arm.

I'm desperate to touch her everywhere. I want to pull the covers off of her and show her how much she is mine. Screw waiting for her to ask me to touch her. What the hell was I thinking saying that?

My beautiful Annabell is laying on her back with her head tilted slightly to the right. She is sleeping so peacefully. She looks so breathtaking, and she smells mouthwatering.

Her dog sits on the end of the bed. She's eating the treat I brought her. I'm hoping this will make us fast friends. Plus, I didn't want her growling at me and waking Annabell up.

Placing a knee onto the bed, I nudge closer to her. She takes a deep breath in as my weight shifts the bed, but thankfully she doesn't wake. That's the good news. The bad news is I got a glimpse of her right nipple. She wants to be touched. That's why she wore this... right?

The t-shirt is the thinnest I have ever seen. It has holes all over it, and it's stretched out. I'm not even sure it's still a shirt anymore. With her movement, it caused her right nipple to stick out, and now I can't take my eyes off of that beautiful pink nipple.

All I can think about is knowing how it would pucker when I touched it. Would it feel soft under my light touch? Would it want to be pinched? Or licked? Or sucked? Or maybe it would want to be nibbled on.

The more and more I watch and think about her, the harder I'm growing. If I don't leave this room right now, I'm going to slide her nipple into my mouth. Maybe she wouldn't feel it. Maybe she wouldn't notice. Maybe I could get away with just one lick.

Leaning down, the smell of her floral shampoo floods my nostrils. My mouth is just one inch away from her *waiting nipple. Just as I'm about to find out what pure happiness tastes like, I hear her say something.*

"Conrad," *she mumbles and I almost combust. She is dreaming about me. Fuck, I don't just want to be a dream. I want to be her reality.*

Standing back up, I walk towards her dresser. Scanning her belongings I spot her necklace she was wearing yesterday. I wonder if it's significant to her? Picking it up, I'm tempted to throw it away. The only necklace I want her to wear is my hand around her neck. And what a beautiful necklace that would make.

Walking into the bathroom, I pause at the toilet. No, I won't be that cruel to her. It might be special. Dropping the necklace onto the counter I walk towards her side table. Quickly, I download the app on her phone that allows me to track her.

You better take this phone with you everywhere you go. Pleased, I head over to the bedroom door. Before I go, I turn back and whisper to her. "Soon, Princess."

Shaking my head, I come back to reality when I see Annabell headed toward Barbara's room.

"Where do you think you're going?" Grabbing the paperwork she needs to fill out for her employment, I slowly head towards her.

"I'm sorry I don't know your name. I will call you Mrs. King for now," I hear her say once I make my way to the door. She's talking to Barbara. If that was actually my mom, this would make me want her even more.

She's kind where I'm evil. She's bright where I'm darkness. She's open where I'm closed off. She's gentle where I'm rough. She's the other part of my soul. The one I have been longing for for too long.

Opening the door, her eyes go wide when she sees me. Surprise is replaced with worry. She thinks I'm going to be mad that she is here. If it had been a couple days ago, I would have been. But now that her medications are working the right way, I want her in here.

"I should leave," she says as she goes to walk past me. I don't move. Her eyes meet mine. They are pleading with me to move out of the way, to end the torture we have so clearly made for each other. But I stand my ground.

"Sit down," I order. She doesn't move. She looks at me for a moment too long.

"Do I really need to repeat myself? We all know how much I enjoy doing that," I continue.

Reluctantly, she takes a seat in the recliner next to the bed. She is trying to ignore me all while obeying me at the same time.

You are too much, Princess. Do you really think I won't correct that attitude?

"Don't be upset, Princess." I walk over towards her and take a seat on the window seat. She watches me intently. Her gaze drops to my lips as I settle right next to her. She's thinking about kissing me.

Just ask me to kiss you, and I will give you everything.

But instead she says, "I'm fine." Which is complete bullshit. She is not fine. She's clearly upset.

"You don't sound fine," I say as I lean back against the window seat. Placing my feet up on the bench so my legs are stretched out, I make sure to brush her bare arm. I immediately see her body react to my touch.

God, this woman was made for me.

The way her body reacts to every touch, look, and close proximity, I know she's mine already.

"What is your mother's name?" Annabell interrupts my thoughts.

"Barbara," I say after a few moments. I guess it's only normal for her to want to know her patient's name. I just hope she doesn't ask too many more questions.

"Barbara King?"

"Yes." I give her a short answer in hopes she will stop with her questions.

"I hope you don't mind me asking questions about her. I like getting to know my patients," she says as she watches Barbara.

"I get it. You may ask questions. It doesn't mean I'll answer them, Princess." I watch her as I say this. Her legs pull together as if she is trying to ease the aching between her legs. If only she knew how much I could help her with that.

"So, what happened to her?" She asks. I'm thankful for the interruption because my mind is running ragged thinking about being between her thighs.

"She had a stroke," I answer with as much ache in my voice as possible. In reality, I couldn't care less about this woman. But I knew this question would come, and I'm glad I had an answer ready for her.

"I'm sorry to hear that. That must have been difficult for you. I can't imagine." She looks at me. Her eyes are full of sympathy. I hate that she is wasting her compassion on this woman.

"Thanks. It was pretty unexpected, but she had a great life. I got to spend a lot of time with her. I know she was happy until the end." I try to give Annabell back the smile in her eyes she once had. Maybe thinking her life was full of happiness, it will bring Annabell joy.

"How does the doctor say she is doing? Are they still coming by to check on her? I haven't seen them at all. Is she still sick?" Annabell fires off question after question. I want to tell her to stop, but I know that will just raise her curiosity.

"They usually come when you are in your room. They say she is doing better, but still needs time before she is out of the woods." She nods her head as she looks back over towards Barbara. I wish I knew what she was thinking. Is she suspicious at all? Can she tell I'm lying? Usually I'm a great liar, but I have a feeling she is going to start seeing right through me.

"So how old are you?" Her question surprises me. Why would she ask me that? One minute we are on the topic of my mother, and now she wants to know my age. Why?

"Why? Do you think I'm old? I ask with a slight grin. To my surprise, she laughs. She actually laughs at my questions. "What's so funny?"

"You are absolutely not old. You're hot." She finally says between laughs. Realizing what she said, she covers her mouth with her hand. She has the hardest time not saying exactly what she is thinking. I like that, and she thinks I'm hot. That's very good to know. I'd have to say, I like these questions much better than the ones about Barbara.

"I'm glad to hear you think I'm hot and not old." I pause for a moment. Should I tell her my real age? What if it scares her off? She is way too young for me, but that's not going to stop me. "I'm thirty-eight." I decided to tell her the truth. I'd like for there to be as many truths between us as possible.

I look over at her to study her reaction. If she is turned off from the fact that I'm 17 years older than her, she doesn't show it.

"You definitely have the body of a twenty-five-year-old. Actually it's way better than a twenty-five-year-old." Her admission makes me grin. If only she knew what this body could do for her. It's way better than anything a twenty-five-year-old could do. Experience has its benefits.

"So, why have you been avoiding me the past two days?" I guess she noticed that. I can't help but grin at her once again. I don't think I have smiled this much in my entire life. It's something about the woman.

"Did you miss me, Princess?" I tease her.

God, I hope she did.

"No. I just think it's incredibly rude of you to disappear for two days," she says, crossing her arms. Did she just call me rude? And look at that attitude she is having. She seriously needs a firm hand, and I would love to give her mine… right on her ass.

"Rude? I didn't realize it was rude for me to be gone for work. Do I detect a hint of bitterness?" I joke with her, but I know she is right. I was avoiding her. It killed me to stay away from her, but if I hadn't…I know I would have lost control. I want her too much. Even sitting here not touching her is killing me.

"No! Absolutely not. That's not what I meant. Never mind. Forget I said anything." She is getting flustered and it's just about the cutest thing I've ever seen. I can't help but pretend like I have no clue what she's talking about.

"So, it was work? What is it that keeps you away for two whole days?" She can't keep her mouth shut, and it's so funny. She is clearly upset about me avoiding her, but she's pretending not to be. And I can't help but laugh. I don't just smirk, I'm over here belly rolling laughing.

"You're adorable, Princess." Her cheeks flush, but she looks away. I can tell she has so much on her mind, but for once she doesn't speak it.

"Since your mom is doing better, I need to start work. I need to make money," she says abruptly.

"If this is about money, I will front you money. That's not a problem. I need you to fill out some paperwork first." I hand her the folder of the employee paperwork I brought in with me.

"I do not want your money unless I have earned it. I will get this filled out and sent to you," she says as she takes the folder. She stands up and heads for the door. Before she leaves, she turns back to me.

"If I can't start soon, I need to leave and find a new job Mr. Conrad." I feel myself start to panic. This is what I was worried about.

"Ms. Annabell," I called after her before she could leave. "Please, don't leave. We need you." I say we but I mean I.

I need you.

I need her to stay. I would be lost if she left. I finally found my one, and I'll be damned if she tries to leave. I'll never let her go. Not even if she asks me to.

"We need you to work for us. We need you to do your job. We will be ready for you very soon. I promise. Please don't worry about money. Everything you need is at your disposal."

"Thank you," she says. Then, she turns on her heels and walks out of the door.

Chapter 23 Conrad

Frustration takes over and I slam my fist against my desk. Two seconds later, there is a knock at my door. "Come in," I call out. I came into the office today after my talk with Annabell. I don't like how things went. I don't want her leaving after I just found her. Does she not understand? Does she not feel the pull between us? I can't be alone in that. I see the way I affect her, but is that just because of my looks? Or is it something deeper? God, I hope it's something deeper.

"Are you alright, Mr. Conrad?" Franchesca asks while lingering in the doorway. She knows not to bother me when I'm in one of my moods, so I'm not sure why she is asking me this right now.

"I'm fine," I yell back.

"Is there anything I can get for you?" I want to say yes. Bring me a lowlife so I can beat the shit out of them and feel their pulse run out under my touch. That always makes me feel better, but I decided that probably isn't in her job description. Though, I bet she would do it for me.

"Maybe a chicken salad sandwich from the deli. I'm trying to get as much work done as I can before 4 pm. I have a meeting I have to get to." There's no meeting other than the meeting I'm going to be having with Annabell.

"Of course, Sir. I'll call them now and have them deliver it. Did you want your spinach and fruit smoothie as well?" Franchesca asks. That does sound pretty good.

"Yes. Thank you Franchesca," I thank her without looking at her. Thankfully, she shuts the door without saying anything else.

Running my hands against the cedar wood on my desk, I can't help but think how it would be to have Annabell splayed out on it. With her feet on the edge. Open wide for my viewing, eating, and fucking.

I feel myself getting hard at the thought. Logging into the home camera, I search for Annabell. She is in her room, sitting criss crossed on her bed as she plays with her dog.

She's so happy. I love seeing that smile on her. I want to be that smile. I want to be the person that puts that smile on her face each and every day. The only time I don't want her smiling is when her eyes are rolling in the back of her head because of me. But either way… it will be because of me.

Once I've had my lunch and shake, I get most of my work finished. I could probably stick around for another hour and make some calls, but I'll have one of the head financial advisors make them. I'm ready to get home and see what my beautiful Princess is doing.

Pulling into the single car bay, I shut the garage door and go into the house from the side door. It's oversized for a single car garage. Honestly, it could fit two cars in there, but I have my work desk on one side. It houses all of the tools I use. And I don't mean DIY tools. I'm talking about my Dexter tools. I don't have many, I prefer to use my bare hands when I end someone's life. The occasional knife comes in handy.

I keep a padlock on the door because I don't want anyone wandering inside and seeing my black duffle bag that has my black clothing and random hunting knives. That wouldn't be too fun to explain.

Heading right to the kitchen, I take off my suit jacket and lay it over one of the bar stools. I need a reason to go see Annabell, and what better of a reason than to bring her an iced coffee.

Walking up the stairs with her coffee in my hand, I hide the straw in my back pocket. Knocking on the door, I lean against the doorframe and wait for her to answer. It takes her a couple of minutes before she swings the door open.

The moment she does, I smile. Those hazel eyes go right to my heart and dick. Without saying a word, I hand her the iced coffee.

"For me?" I nod and smirk at her. Pulling the straw out from behind my back, I slide it into the drink. I can see her trying to muffle her smile.

"Thank you, Mr. Conrad. That was very kind of you," she says as she takes a sip. I can tell she is being very careful not to suck seductively on the straw, but honestly…I'm just torturing myself with even giving her that straw.

"Here are those papers, Mr. Conrad," she says as she hands me the paperwork. When she does, my hand touches hers. I feel fire in my veins. I want to grab her and pull her into me. Even touching her hand has me on edge, so I pull away.

"I didn't need the hard copies, but thank you. I'll put these in your file." Her mouth slightly drops open, and I'm not exactly sure why. But it has me stepping towards her.

"You might want to close that pretty mouth of yours, Princess. There's no telling what might make its way into it," I say as I imagine sliding many parts of my body into her open mouth.

She nods her head and thanks me. Though, I'm not sure what she is thanking me for. I'd be happy to watch her thank me while she is on her knees.

She bites her lip as she watches me. Pure, absolute torture. I know she's thinking the exact same filthy thoughts as I am. She is just too shy to tell me about them.

"I bet I can guess what you're thinking, Princess." I take another step closer because why the hell not jump right into the fire. I'm already burnt.

"I'm not sure what you mean?" Oh how cute. She's playing coy again. Has she not learned by now?

"Don't be coy with me." I'm no longer leaning against the doorframe. I have made my way into the bedroom. The bedroom that smells just like her. The bedroom where I sneak in at night and watch her. The bedroom where she moans my name in her sleep.

"One day, you will beg me to touch you. You will beg me to throw your legs around my head, to feel my lips all over you. You're not ready yet. I know that, but one day you will be, and I will be ready for you, Princess."

She clutches onto the glass as if it's going to help her stand up. I can see her legs start to shake. She's bothered by my close proximity. I try not to show that she too affects me, but if she felt how hard I was for her right now. There would never be a question whether I wanted her or not.

Without saying another word, I leave her room and head back downstairs before I go too far.

Turning my head, I hear the back door shut. Was that Annabell? She didn't feel like sharing where she was going tonight? I'm not so sure how I feel about her leaving the house so late. Scratch that, I hate that she is leaving the house so late. Granted, it isn't even eight o'clock.

Where do you think you're going, Princess?

Switching my laptop over to the cameras in her room, I rewind them a little. I see her standing in front of her mirror dressed in the sexiest dress I've ever seen, and she isn't with me.

Pulling up the tracker app on my phone, I watch where she goes. Impatient, I go outside to see if her car is still in the driveway. "Damnit," I growl when I see her car is still here. Either someone picked her up, or she took an Uber so she could drink. And I do not like the thought of either one.

Rushing upstairs, I grab some clothes out of my closet and dress as quickly as I can. Checking my mirror to make sure my hair is acceptable, I slide into my shoes. I'm sure she has reached her destination by now.

Pulling out my phone I see she is at the restaurant, Steller Fam. Grabbing my keys, I head to the restaurant. She is going to learn, she can't go anywhere without me knowing.

Walking up to the restaurant, I spot her at the bar through the window. My jaw nearly hits the floor. I've turned into a wuss, drooling after his woman, and I don't even care. Her legs are a mile long in those heels as she sits on the stool with her legs crossed. That's the necklace I want to wear. Her two legs wrapped around my neck as I bury my face between them.

After remembering where I am and what I'm doing here, I grab a seat at one of the outside tables. I don't want her to notice me coming inside. I can still see her, but she can't see me. She's with another woman. I'm assuming that's her friend.

Good. I would have lost my shit if she was out with a guy. I wouldn't have cared how I looked. I would have walked over to him and punched him. If he touched her, I would chop his hands off.

She's mine.

After they finish eating and drinking their drinks, they hop out of the stools and make their way outside. I lift up the menu to cover my face. Instead of calling for an Uber to take them home…I see them starting to walk down the road.

Where the fuck are you going dressed like that and alone?

I give them a head start even though I want to grab her by the hair and pull her into my truck. It's not safe for two attractive women to be walking alone, at night, and in the city. Good thing I'm here to watch over her. You never know what kind of evil might be lurking just around the corner.

Following them all the way to club Empire, I'm seething by the time I walk into the door. This was your plan, Princess? To go clubbing? You don't belong here. You belong at home, with me.

I've been here a couple of times. The owner is actually one of my clients, so we have had several meetings here in both the daytime and nighttime. I know the club pretty well.

The bouncer at the door recognizes me immediately. "Conrad, what are you doing here?"

"My girl just went in with her friend. I'm meeting her inside," I tell him with a nod.

"Your girl? She's a lucky lady." He moves the rope so I can go inside.

"I'm the lucky one. Thanks." I'm greeted by loud music. It needs to be turned down a couple of notches. It's way too loud to hear someone let alone think.

I make my rounds and show my face to the owner. Since the bouncer saw me, I know he will tell him. I really don't feel like chatting about work, but it needed to be done. And now that that's out of the way... I can go find my one.

After a full walk through, I spot her on the dance floor... with a guy.

What the actual fuck?

He slides behind her and grinds against her ass. The pounding in my ears isn't from the music. It's from the blood rushing to my brain. The anger I feel when I see him slide his arm around her front and pull her even closer to him is unbearable. I'm seeing red and it's not the good kind.

She tries to pull away from him, but his grip tightens making it impossible to escape his grasp. Lucky for her, I'm here.

Yup, this guy is going to die.

Unable to stand idle any longer, I walk up to the guy behind her. Having to remind myself not to kill him right in the middle of this club, I rip him away from her. He stumbles so far back, he's no longer on the dance floor.

Looking back at him, it seems as if he is about to protest, but then he sees the murderous expression in my eyes.

Your life ends tonight regardless. Depending on what you do now will determine how much I drag it out.

He places his hands in the air as if to surrender.

Good choice.

Grabbing Annabell's arm, I pull her down the private hall that leads to several offices. The bouncer doesn't even bat an eye as I drag her into a private room. Shutting the door behind us, I spin her around to face me. Her eyes are full of shock and relief at the same time. I guess the fear that a stranger just took her into a private room wasn't lost on her.

"What are you doing here?"

"I could ask you the same thing." I could also ask why the fuck you were letting some guy touch you that wasn't me. The anger burns at my skin. I'm trying to hold it at bay, but it's getting harder and harder the more I think about it.

"Are you here for me?" She asks as if she's completely innocent.

"Of course I'm here for you." Why else would I be here in this room with her? Her stance waivers as I take a step closer to her. She rests against the wall behind her as she stares up at me. I know she wants me, but I'm not going to give into her just yet. I plan on winning. I plan on hearing her beg me before I give in.

"Ms. Annabell, I think it's time for you to go home," I say as I look down at her emerald dress. It's a fuck me dress, and I want nothing more than to oblige. She doesn't seem to be able to reply, so I continue taking her in.

Her heels make her four inches taller than she actually is. Her legs look even longer standing up, and the dress leaves little to the imagination. I don't blame that guy for wanting what's mine.

Stepping so close to her, I can feel her tits against my chest. My dick instantly hardens. I should drop to my knees, pull one of her legs over my shoulder and taste what I'm doing to her right now.

Fuck.

Placing my left hand against the wall, I lean down to whisper against her ear. "That dress has me wanting to break my own rules, Princess."

"What rules?" Her breath comes out in pants.

"The one where I said I wouldn't touch you until you begged me to touch you, but right now I want to forget

I ever said that." Allowing my gaze to scan her body once more, I find her eyes again.

"You're going to cause me trouble, Princess. I can already tell." The way her legs start to shake has me itching to get her off her feet and onto her back.

"I won't be a bad kind of trouble, Mr Conrad. I will be great at my job and I'm sure we will have fun together," she says looking away. How can she be so fucking hot and cute at the same time? I'm not sure my heart can take this.

"More than you know. Now go get your friend and let's go home." She pouts for a moment, but eventually does as she is told.

Heading out to grab her friend, Annabell stumbles. I place my arms around her waist to steady her. The moment my hand touches her bare back, I have to bite back a moan. Her skin is like silk where mine is like steel.

"Allison, we need to go," I hear Annabell yell into her friend's ear. Allison is it? Was this club your suggestion Allison?

As soon as Allison turns to face us, her eyes zoom over to me. "Oh my gosh, Annabell. Nice work. See, now you can get your mind off of your boss for a night." Her comment has me both smiling and staring daggers into her friend.

For one, I can't believe Annabell told her about me. I'm glad she's thinking about me. Secondly, what the fuck? Why is she encouraging my one to go find some other guy so she can forget about me?

Annabell shakes her head in hopes to get her friend to stop talking. She is unsuccessful. She leans down and whispers into her ear.

"Oh shit. He's the boss? No wonder you got it so bad girl. He is hoooooooot," she says, dragging out the o. I guess that's a little better than her thinking I'm some random guy trying to get into Annabell's pants. I'll kill every mother fucker that tries.

She's mine.

My grip tightens around her waist. "Let's go," I say to them both. Thankfully, neither of them protest.

Once we make it into my truck, Allison gives me her address. She climbs in the back seat and passes out almost immediately. Opening the door for Annabell, I help her into my truck. "You need to buckle up," I say as I lean over and buckle her seatbelt unbearably slowly.

Hearing the click, I slowly drag my hand across the belt. Skimming her lap as I do, I watch her breathing pick up once again. "Thank you." Her voice comes out as a whisper and it's all I can do not to kiss her. She's so close. And she's biting her lip.

Dammit to hell.

I close her door and head to the driver's side of the truck. The whole way over I remind myself not to touch her.

Don't fuck her in the truck. Don't fuck her in the truck. Dont' fuck her in the truck.

But it's no help because as soon as I settle into the truck and start the drive back to the mansion, Annabell's dress has ridden up. And her legs have parted slightly. Is she trying to get me to fuck her? Or does she not know what she's doing to me?

With both hands, I'm gripping the steering wheel so tightly my fingers hurt. I'm hoping the harder I squeeze, the harder it will be to let go and give in. I can't take watching her like this, and not being able to touch her.

"You better pull that dress down and close those legs before I take advantage of your drunken state. And trust me, I'm not above doing so," I growl. Her eyes are wide with surprise. Grabbing the hem of her dress, she pulls it down as much as possible as she closes her legs.

Pulling my focus back to the road, part of me was hoping she wouldn't pull her dress down. Then, maybe I would have had an excuse to touch her again.

I picture myself reaching over and sliding my hand between her parted legs. Making her moan so loud she wakes up her friend. Then, I'd pull her over and make her suck my dick until my cum drove down her throat.

I have got to get ahold of myself.

Adjusting my now very hard dick, I try to focus on anything but the building sexual tension that's happening between us.

"What if I hadn't closed my legs?" I hear a whisper. Did she seriously just ask me that? Does she not know I am about to explode? Does she not know you shouldn't play with fire?

Gripping the steering wheel even harder, I look at her for a brief moment. Her eyes are hooded just like mine. "Then I would have told you to pull your dress up so I could see."

She bites her lip at my answer. If only she knew what I really wanted to do to her. She probably wouldn't have asked me that.

To my utter shock, she pulls the edge of her dress up. I can see the edge of her underwear, and my mouth is actually watering. I'm going to wreck. I should pull over, but I need to get her friend home.

"Annabell." I warn her. She leans her head back against the headrest and runs her left hand up her leg.

"Fuck, Princess," I say as my own breath starts to become uneven. She's teasing me. "Pull it up more. I want it around your hips."

She does as she's told and slowly pulls the dress up around her hips. I can see the black lace panties hugging her porcelain skin. It's such a beautiful contrast.

Pulling up to Allison's apartment, I park right in front of her door. Looking over at Annabell, her eyes are starting to droop. I better make this fast. "I'm going to take her in. Do not move. Do you understand? I want you just like this when I return." She nods in understanding.

Grabbing Allison from the back of the truck, I carry her to her door. Managing to get the door unlocked and not dropping her, I lay her on her couch. Locking her door, I hide the key under her mat. I'll have to make sure Annabell lets her know.

As soon as I get back into the truck, my dick cries. Annabell has fallen fast asleep, with her dress resting around her waist.

She's absolutely beautiful. Though I'm dying on the inside, I'm glad she is resting. "Our time will come soon, Princess."

Chapter 24 Annabell

I can't stop watching him as he drives us home. I can't stop thinking about what he said. *"You better pull that dress down and close those legs before I take advantage of your drunken state. And trust me, I'm not above doing so."*

Without thinking, I pulled my dress down and closed my legs, but now I'm wishing I hadn't. What would he have done? Would he have touched me? I imagine him sliding his hand between my legs to get to what he wants.

"What if I hadn't closed my legs?" Oh my gosh. Did I just ask that? I guess I'm more drunk than I thought I was. Mr. Conrad looks over at me as if he is ready to eat me.

"Then I would have told you to pull your dress up so I could see." Hearing his words…I do just that. Pulling my dress back up so he can see just the edge of my panties, I bite my lip as he takes in the site.

"Annabell," he warns me. I know I'm playing with fire, but at this point I don't care if I get burnt. I'm tired of waiting. I just want his hands on me.

"Fuck, Princess." I can tell he is about to break. Good, I want him to.

"Pull it up more. I want it around your hips," he growls while gripping the steering wheel so hard his knuckles are turning white.

Pulling my dress up over my hips, I allow it to pool at my waist. His eyes burn into my skin, and I love the feeling of it. I never want him to look away.

The truck comes to a stop, and I realize we are at Allison's apartment.

"I'm going to take her in. Do not move. Do you understand? I want you just like this when I return." I nod as I watch him scoop her up and carry her to her door. I lean my head against the window as I watch him unlock her door and carry her at the same time.

God, he must be incredibly strong.

They disappear into her apartment, and my eyes close as I wait for him to return.

Feeling his arms around me, he carries me upstairs. I'm partially awake, but I let my dream state remain. I don't want to wake up right now. I'm enjoying his arms around me too much. I don't want it to end. He makes me feel safe. He makes me feel desired like I've never felt before.

I must have forgotten to lock my door because he lets himself into my bedroom. Laying me on my bed, he disappears into my closet. Emerging, he holds a t-shirt in his hands.

"Sit up," he orders me. With little control over my body, I do my best to help him undress me. If I wasn't so drunk, I would be very aware of how naked I am in front of him right now. But I don't care at the moment.

Somehow I'm stripped of my dress, covered in a t-shirt, and alone in my bed before I even know what happened. Unable to process much, I roll over and quickly slip back into my dream state.

Chapter 25 Conrad

I've been tossing and turning since I put Annabell to bed. It took everything I had not to try anything. She was so vulnerable, so naked, and so mine. But I covered her up and put her to bed.

My dick has been getting in the way all night. I don't even have the desire to rub one out. I just want her. I just want to bury myself in her and stay there for eternity. It's where I belong.

It's close to four in the morning. I got home about an hour ago from taking care of that son of a bitch from the club. He was still wandering around the club when I made my way back. I thought about cutting him a break. Maybe he didn't deserve to die for dancing with my one, but when I see him…all of the rage comes back.

"Why are you doing this man?" The pussy cries after I punch him for the tenth time.

"You don't remember me? Well, I'm deeply offended," I say as I deliver another blow.

"I thought we had something back in the club," I say as I continue punching him. I always wear gloves so I don't fuck up my hands. It's kind of hard to explain that away.

"I'm sorry man, I didn't know that was your girl. She didn't say anything." Just because she didn't say anything doesn't give you permission to put your hands on what's mine. Fucking idiot.

He's knocked out by my last blow. Laying on the floor limp, I drag him over to the tarp I left out just for him. "Goodbye buddy. It was nice talking with you."

Slipping the knife through his carotid artery, It only takes moments for him to bleed out.

"No, where are you going? Why are you leaving me?" I shake my head as I remember where I am. Was that Annabell?

Jumping out of bed, I sprint to her room. Is someone in her room with her? I'll kill whoever is with her.

When I open her door, I see her on her bed. She's alone, but she is fighting with the covers. She's having a nightmare.

"Conrad," she cries. Hearing the agony in her voice, I ran to her. Sitting on the bed I try to wake her.

"Annabell." She doesn't wake up.

"Annabell, you're alright." Her eyes spring open, and they land on me. She's watching me as if she is seeking comfort. I want to give that to her. I want her to always seek me out.

Realizing my hands are gripping both of her shoulders, I quickly release her.

"I'm sorry. I um, I was just trying to get you to wake up," I stumble over my words. I feel ridiculous apologizing for touching her. Just a few hours ago, I carried her up the stairs and undressed her. But she is fully awake right now. I don't want her thinking I'm not a man of my word.

"What are you sorry for?" She almost seems annoyed.

"I told you I wouldn't touch you until you asked me to. You didn't ask, so I'm sorry." I'm tired of saying the same thing over and over again.

Dammit woman, when are you going to beg me to touch you?

I watch her as her mind processes things. My hands that were once on her shoulders are now on either side of her body. I'm instinctively bent over her. I'm begging her to let go. I see how close she is. She wants to get lost in me. She wants to give up control, and I'm ready to take it.

Reaching up, she cups my face. The sudden warmth of her hand has every nerve in my body exposed. It's as if they have opened up to get an even closer feel. Her thumb traces the bottom of my lip. Without thinking, I pull her thumb into my mouth. I have to taste her.

Running my tongue along her thumb, I can taste her on me. Every taste bud in my mouth is jumping for joy at this very moment. She lets out a whimper, and I'm about to lose my shit.

"Kiss me. Please," I hear her whisper. All the hair on my body stands at attention.

Finally, thank God.

I don't waste any time. I need to have her against me. I need to feel her lips. I need it as much as I need this air in my lungs. But I'd gladly give it up to feel her lips just once.

Grabbing her face between my hands, I crushed her lips against mine. I'm flung out into oblivion the moment her lips touch mine. It's an impossible feeling. One I never would have expected.

I'm not gentle. There is too much built up tension to be gentle. Reluctantly, I release her, but only for a moment. I need to be closer to her. Ripping the covers off of her, I crawl on top of her. She opens her legs for me as I settle between them.

Feeling the heat between her legs as I settle over her, I groan. My lips can't get back to her fast enough. I'm hungry for her. I haven't eaten like this in thirty-eight years, and I'm a starved man.

I move my kisses down her neck because I'm greedy, and I need to feel all of her. If there was a way to kiss her lips, neck, tits, and pussy at the same time…. Dammit I'd be doing it right now.

Rocking my hips against her core, she lets out a delicious moan. God, it feels amazing. My dick is home, and I haven't even been inside of her yet. "You can't be making those sounds if you want me to stay in control of myself, Princess." I plan on getting her off tonight, I plan on making her scream my name, but I'm not going to fuck her tonight.

She moans again and this time it goes straight to my dick. It's fully erect and ready to play. It's going to take everything in me not to strip her down and fuck her. "Dammit, Princess."

I bite her neck in response. She is already driving me crazy, and I've only had a taste. The noises that come from her are perfect. I want to make a mixtape of them and play them over and over. Of course, I'd never get any work done. I don't know how I'm going to get work done now that I've had her against my lips. I may need to take a leave of absence.

Needing to taste more of her, I forcibly pull her shirt up exposing her beautiful breasts. I could look at them all day, but right now I'm desperate to taste them. I'm desperate to feel them harden against my teeth. Pulling one into my mouth, my tongue dances over her nipple until it beads up for me.

Growing impatient, I move to the other side and suck her other nipple into my mouth. Though I am enjoying these kisses, my fingers itch to be stained with her scent. I slowly run my hand down her flat stomach.

One day I'll put a baby in there.

Dipping my fingers into her panties, I feel her stiffen. She's just as ready for this as I am. I can smell her arousal already, and it's the sweetest smell. Not wasting my time, I find that beautiful ball of nerves and show it the attention it so much deserves.

"Oh, Conrad." My name rolls off her tongue like honey. Feeling her wetness pour out of her, and it's all for me.

"That's it, Princess. Show me how badly you want me," I growl into her ear as I suck on her ear lobe.

I continue my torture on her clit. The sound of her wetness rolling between my fingers has me so hard it hurts. She's this wet for me. She is coming apart at my hands, for me. I've wanted this for so long. I've dreamt of this for years. She's finally here, in my arms, screaming my name.

And that's exactly what she does. Her orgasm hits her like a brick wall. As I suck on her nipple and continue to roll my fingers against her, she rides the waves until they are simply aftershocks.

I bury my face against her neck as my hand stills. Not wanting to move, I lay there against her listening to her raising heart. It's matching the beat of mine. Two hearts now beat as one.

"You're such a good girl. I could watch you do that all day. Your body responds to me so well. Just as it should." I knew it would. I knew she was perfect. I knew she was my one the moment I saw her.

Reluctantly, I pull my hand from her underwear. Kissing her lips, I relish this feeling. "I can't get enough of these lips."

"Mmm, neither can I," she says as she reaches for my head. Releasing her lips, I dodge her grasp and roll to the side of her.

Grabbing her, I pull her against my chest. "Close your eyes, Princess." Surprisingly, she doesn't fight me. She stills beside me as she starts to drift back to sleep. After the orgasm she just had, I imagine she is pretty tired.

Nuzzling her closer to me, I whisper to her. "There will be much more. You get your rest, little one. You are going to need it now that you're mine."

Chapter 26 Conrad

Waking with my arms wrapped around Annabell is pure joy. The world makes sense now. The sun shines brighter. The birds sound softer. I hate to sound so sappy, but dammit this girl has changed me. She is everything I was missing.

I didn't want to sneak out at six this morning, but Barbara needed her medication. I didn't want to miss that and have her waking up on me. That would be difficult to explain.

Putting on my clothes, I get ready to head downstairs when I hear creaking coming from the stairs. Peering out of my door, I look over towards Annabell's room. Her door is open. I know I closed it when I stepped out this morning. Maybe she wanted it open in hopes I would come back.

Should I go check on her?

Looking into her bedroom, I see her bathroom light on. She must have opened it, I don't see anyone else here. Good thinking because it's too early to hide a dead body this morning. I didn't get enough sleep. If no one else opened the door, why would she leave the door open? Isn't she worried her dog will escape?

Seeing her dog standing at the edge of the bed, I make my way down to my office. Something isn't sitting right with me.

Logging onto my laptop, I click on the camera set up in Annabell's bedroom. Rewinding the feed until I see the door open to her bedroom, I pause it. The angle of my camera can't see it.

Dammit!

Watching her room, I see her come out of the bathroom. She seems fine. Her dog seems normal. Maybe my dark mind goes to the worst thing. Or maybe I'm right on point and I just don't realize it.

Keeping the laptop open, I bring it with me to the home gym. Setting it on the bar, I start my run. By the time I'm finished running and lifting weights, it's close to seven.

Lugging the laptop back to my office, I look for Annabell. She's still in bed so I decide to take a quick shower. Walking by her room, the door is now shut. I want to go in and wrap my arms around her and never leave this house, but I really need to shower.

Showering as quickly as I can, I get dressed and make my way down to the kitchen. Just as I make my way into the living room, I hear a noise in the kitchen. When I round the corner, I see the most beautiful body trying to make coffee.

"Good morning, Princess. How did you sleep?" I ask, startling her. As soon as she turns around, I'm greeted with the best smile. I guess she's as happy to see me as I am to see her.

Seeing her in her sleep shirt has me growing hard already and it's not even eight am. Lifting my fingers to my nose, I'm sad to realize I can no longer smell her. We're going to have to rectify that soon.

"I slept very well thank you," she says as her cheeks blush. I can't get enough of the way I affect her. I love seeing her turn to putty in my hands.

"Did it have anything to do with me?" I don't have to wait anymore to touch her. I can take her right here if I want, but I love watching her shake. Taking a step closer, I watch her intently.

"I'm not sure what you mean." She's playing coy. Has she not learned yet? I always get what I want.

Stepping even closer to her, I inhale her scent. I'm only inches away from her now. "Did you need me to remind you already, Princess? Because I'd love to remind you several times a day." That is the dream. To fuck her several times a day. If I could live off of her alone, I would be a very hearty man.

"You don't think we should keep things professional? I might have lost myself a little bit last night," she says innocently. This woman has got to be shitting me. I know she's just messing with me, but if she thinks I would ever let her go back to not spreading her legs for me...she has another thing coming. Doesn't she know...she's mine.

"Fuck that! You're mine now, Princess. You better stop running from me because I will always find you. I will always be there watching you." She doesn't know it yet, but I really mean it. I will always find her, and I WILL always be watching her. Even if she tries to leave me...I'll drag her back to her rightful place.

"Yours?" She questions as she raises her eyebrow. Is she challenging me? Does she not understand when I say mine, I mean MINE.

Taking a step closer to her because I need to get my point across. "Yes! MINE," I say as I grab a handful of her hair and repeat, "Mine."

I feel her body give into me, and it's a glorious feeling.

Yes, give in to me. You might as well. You have no other choice.

I hold her close with her hair still balled in my fist. Looking down at her, I feel a sense of pride. This girl….is mine.

Looking back up at me, she smiles and whispers, "Yes, Sir."

Unable to resist any longer, I pull her against my lips. Feeling that familiar tingle throughout my body, I devour her. Not taking her lightly, my tongue invades her mouth. Running my tongue against her, it makes me want to take her to bed and see how that tongue looks on my dick. But instead, I pull away.

"I have to run out for a bit, but when I return I will come find you, and I will show you what I mean by *mine*." I kiss her one more time. I kiss her so she remembers whos she is. I kiss her so she still feels me against her even hours after I have left.

"Please." Seeing the desire in her eyes has me wanting to change my plan, but I have an important business meeting in the office that I cannot miss.

"I'm going to send you a text, that way you have my number."

"Be good and give my mother some space today. The doctors will be here to check on her, so you do not need to go in and see her." I give her a very serious look. I should be back in time to give her the medication she needs. I may have to stop by on my lunch break though.

"You got it, boss," she says with a cute little smirk.

"I knew you'd be the right one. I knew it the moment I saw you," I bend down and whisper into her ear. Then, I turn and walk out of the door.

Grabbing my phone, I send her a quick text before I jump into my truck.

Conrad: The only number you will ever need again.

I'm having the hardest time focusing on my meeting. Annabell hasn't texted me back, and I don't understand why. It's driving me crazy. Did she not get my message? I want to walk out of my meeting, drive home, grab her, and throw her over my shoulder. She deserves a beautiful little beating for ignoring me.

I've had to ask the investor to repeat his question twice. I have got to get it together. I can't be making mistakes like this at work. Franchesca has been looking at me like I'm a stranger. If only you knew what has gotten into me…. Or what I'm about to get into.

The thought of getting to be deep inside of Annabell later tonight has me growing hard in my important meeting. Thankfully, I'm behind my desk.

Fuck my mind.

Feeling my watch buzz, I quickly check it and see it's from Annabell. I pull my phone out of my pocket so quickly, I almost drop it.

Get it together, Conrad.

Annabell: You may not be the ONLY one.

I want to reply right away, but I can't be that rude to this investor. Biding my time, I listen as best as I can then ask to break for lunch. Everyone disperses. Once I'm left alone, I'm finally able to respond.

Conrad: Who else could you possibly need?

I wait, but she doesn't respond right away. Where is she?

Conrad: ?

Annabell: 911 perhaps?

I can't help but laugh. Good thing I'm alone.

Conrad: I can rescue you princess. In fact, that's what I'm here for.

Annabell: Do you know CPR?

Conrad: I know mouth-to-mouth.

Conrad: That's what's truly important.

Annabell: Maybe you could teach it to me. You know, just in case.

Conrad: I like the way you think. I will be home soon, and I'll be more than happy to teach you anything you want, princess. All you have to do is ask.

Annabell: I thought I was done asking?

Oh she's right, but I still would enjoy seeing her beg me. I'd still love to teach her a few things.

Conrad: I had promised you I wouldn't touch you until you asked. You asked so now you are mine. But if there is something new, you want me to teach you then I want you to ask me.

Annabell: Like what?

I love that she asked. I love how curious she is. She wants to learn what I like. And there is one thing that I cannot get out of my head.

Conrad: Like if you want me to teach you how to deep throat my dick.

Because I really hope you want to learn that. I want to slide my dick down that beautiful throat of yours. I want to hear you gag on my thick, throbbing dick.

Dammit, now I'm hard again.

Annabell: OK.

Conrad: Don't just say OK. I need you to respond with more anytime you text me.

Annabell: Sorry. I would love for you to teach me what you like.

Conrad: Good, Princess. I will be home in a few hours. You should be ready for me. It will be a long night.

My dick stirs with excitement. It's been suffering without pussy for far too long.

Yes, you finally get your turn.

Chapter 27 Conrad

Annabell: Do you know when you will be home? No rush, I just may have to step out for a moment.

I read the text Annabell must have sent while I was still in my meeting. It was a hell of a day. One I don't care to repeat for a while.

Conrad: I'm headed home. Sorry it was a late night. Are you back at the house?

I'm surprised when I don't get a response right away.

Rushing home, I cannot wait to have Annabell in my arms. It's later than I anticipated. I couldn't even leave for lunch. I had to get Zeak to sneak into the house and give Barbara her medication. Thankfully, he doesn't ask questions. He is a great employee.

"Annabell." I call out to her as soon as I open the door, but I don't get an answer.

Where are you, Princess?

Heading to her room, I see the door is locked. She must not be there. Maybe she's in my room. I can picture her waiting on my bed open for me, waiting like I instructed her to.

Opening my door, I turn on the lights. Instead of seeing a waiting Annabell, I simply see my bed perfectly made.

Pulling out my phone, I text her.

Conrad: Where are you?

No answer.

Conrad: Hello?

I wait five minutes this time, and still nothing. I start pacing my bedroom. Running down stairs, I look to see if her car is here. Gone.

Where the hell are you?

Conrad: Annabell!

I'm starting to lose my patience. Pulling up the app I use to track her phone, I find where she is.

Why the fuck is she at her old apartment.

Conrad: I called several times. Where are you?

I'm about to drive over there. If that dick of an ex-boyfriend still lives there…I'm going to lose my shit.

Why would she go there?

Dialing Zeak's number, he answers on the first ring. "Late one, boss?"

"Yes! I need you to hack into Annabell's phone and see what her last texts were. Send them to me ASAP," I order.

"You got it."

We both hang up without a goodbye. He knows this is serious. I wouldn't be calling and asking this if it wasn't.

Ten minutes later, I get an email from Zeak. I click on it so fast, I nearly break my phone. And what I read makes me want to.

Eric: Anne, we need to talk. Can you come over?
Annabell: No
Eric: Please. I need to talk to you about something. It's an emergency.
Eric: Anne, please. I promise I will explain when you get here. I would really appreciate this.
Eric: Are you coming? I really need you.
Annabell: This better be important. I'll be there in 15.

Conrad: Come home NOW!

My blood is boiling. Why would she go over to see him? Zeak also sent me her recent call log. Apparently she called Allison before she went over there.

What is going on?

Just as I'm about to call her, Zeak sends me another email. It's a text message that was just sent from Annabell's phone to Allison.

Annabell: I should have listened to you. It wasn't an emergency. It wasn't about the apartment. He basically tricked me into going over so he could force himself on me. I'm fine. I got away after I bit his lip. And he slapped me. I cannot believe he put his hands on me like that. I'll fill you in more later. Mr. Conrad has texted me several times. He is probably pissed. Night.

He tried to force himself on her? He slapped her? The fact that she bit his lip means he had his lips on her.

I will cut them from his body. I will make sure he never touches her again.

The rage I'm feeling right now is one I have never felt before. Not only did he touch what was mine, but he did it even after she wanted him to stop. He tried to force himself on her. He slapped her, and he will pay for this.

Hearing the side door open, I take a deep breath and sit down on the elbow of the couch. Deep breath after deep breath, I try to calm myself. I'm murderous right now. I'm angry at Annabell for putting herself in that kind of situation, but I'm also wanting to wrap my arms around her. But I can't let her know I know all most of the details of what happened. If she wants to tell me, I will listen. If she doesn't, then I will have to accept that.

I'm full of anger, but the moment I see her it all fades. I just want to hold her. The thought of losing her overtakes any anger I might have had. But I also can't allow her to know I know. It's a fine line I have to walk.

Putting down my phone, I watch her. She looks at me as if she is worried.

Good. You should be worried.

She licks her lips and I instinctively react to her. My body still wants to fuck her even though I know that's not what she needs. Her eyes flicker to the stairs. Is she really thinking about trying to go upstairs right now? There is no way I'm going to allow that. No matter the situation.

"Sit," I order as I walk over toward her and sit on the sectional closer to her. Thankfully, she doesn't argue. She sits down right beside me. Our legs touch as she relaxes into the couch.

"Where have you been?" I barely get the question out before she starts apologizing.

"I'm so sorry. When I didn't hear from you, I had to run out for a moment. I thought I would be able to make it back in time. I'm really sorry." Small tears start to run down her porcelain skin, and it breaks my heart.

Tilting her head so I can get a better view of her, "Why are you crying, Princess?" Someone this beautiful should not be crying. Much less crying because of a crappy situation she had to deal with. It's not right, and I cannot wait to rectify the situation.

My fingers itch to wrap around his throat. To see the life drain from his eyes as I tell him exactly who I am, it will be a treat to see. But I can't focus on that right now. I need to give Annabell all of my attention.

She covers her face. She's trying to hide from me. I don't ever want her to hide from me. "Tell me what's wrong."

Grabbing both of her thighs, I hoist her on top of my lap. I want her close. I want to care for her. Once she opens her eyes and looks at me, she is straddling me.

This is where you belong, Princess.

"I know you're not going to want to do this, but can you please, just for tonight, pretend I'm fine," she whispers against my chest.

That's the last thing I want to do, she's right. But it's the only thing I can do. It's what she needs, and I plan to give her everything she wants and needs.

Feeling her against my chest, I wrap my arms around her back and pull her closer to me. I can't help but be selfish and want her closer to me. Her breathing has evened out, and we sit in silence for at least twenty minutes. I know she's asleep, but I'm not ready to move her yet. I know as soon as I move her, I will have to leave her. I know this because I won't be able to keep myself from placing her in my bed and finding the guy who hurt her. There is nothing that will stop me from ending his life. No amount of pleading. No amount of moral consciousness. The reaper is coming, and you better get ready.

Carrying her upstairs, I enter my bedroom. Very carefully, I pull back my covers and slide her into my bed. Removing her shoes and dress, I bite my lip when I see the lingerie she wore for me. "Dammit," I whisper. Leaving her there for a moment, I grab one of my t-shirts for her. Slowly placing it over her head, I want my scent on her. I want her here when I return. I want her to feel safe if she does wake up in the middle of the night. I want her to know I cared enough to keep her close by.

Covering her back up, I give her a kiss and close the door. Walking by her room, I hear her dog whining. I can tell she is worried about her human. I can appreciate that. I remember how Rox used to be.

Opening her door, I get down on her level and pet her. "Your mom is fine. She is staying with me tonight. She will let you out in the morning. Are you good with that?" I ask her. I'm met with a wagging tail, so I will take that as approval.

"Now I have to go do away with a bad man that hurt your mom tonight. We can't have that now can we?" Petting her one more time, I usher her back into the room.

"Go to sleep, I'll let you out when I get back." With that I close Annabell's bedroom door. Thankfully, she doesn't whine. I can't handle when dogs whine. It's like my kryptonite. I don't know what I'm going to do when mine and Annabell's baby cries. I'm going to be putty in their hands for sure. I'll be screwed if it's a girl.

Smiling at the thought of our baby girl, I make my way to my office. Grabbing my keys off my desk, I make my way to the garage. Unlocking the padlock, I close the door behind me. I quickly gather all of the supplies I may need and toss them into my truck. I make sure I have my entire truck covered in plastic. I have a feeling this one is going to be a messy one. I plan on taking my time with him.

I leave my phone on the work table. I don't want it to be tracked. Locking the padlock, I head back inside to make sure the house is locked up before I leave. Once I'm satisfied, I make my way around to my truck. With the angel of death going before me, I head to my destination.

My pulse quickens as I park my truck in the alleyway behind his apartment. I'm taking this guy from his home, so I can't have anyone seeing me. It may be rash, but it has to happen tonight. He doesn't deserve to live one more night. And Annabell doesn't deserve to have to be reminded.

Double checking for cameras, I slowly exit my truck when I see the coast is clear. Thankfully, Zeak looked into the cameras along this alley for me already. Lucky for me, the idiots that built this place were lazy and only put some in the front of the building. Unlucky for Eric though.

Putting on the work coveralls and ball cap, I make my way towards his door. With the tarp tucked under my arm, I scan the street. Thankfully, it's pretty bare at this time of night. I plan to allow the body to be discovered, so it can't lead back to me.

Feeling my brow start to sweat, I take a couple of deep breaths. Not only am I anxious, I'm excited as fuck. Ducking into the shadows when I hear someone open their door, I stay hidden in the shadows for a moment longer. It's where I thrive.

Hearing the crunch of twigs below my feet as I make it behind his apartment, it reminds me of what I'm going to do to Eric. Every bone that played a part in touching Annabell will be broken. Every piece of skin that touched her will be removed. He will wish he had never been born by the time I'm done with him.

He lives in a fairly nice quadplex which pisses me off even more knowing that he kicked Annabell out and made her live in a dump. Pulling out the syringe of paralytics I used on Barbara, I quietly pick the lock on his back door. As soon as I hear the lock click, I slide it into my back pocket.

Bracing myself, I enter the apartment. He should be asleep, but I'm always aware of my surroundings. Scanning the house, I don't see him right away. I pull out a small red flashlight. On the off chance someone is outside, it's harder to detect from outside.

Squatting down when I round the corner of the bedroom, I quietly walk closer to the bed. Getting the needle into position, I make sure it's ready to dive into his neck. Just as I'm about to lunge, I realize he isn't there.

Dammit. Where is he?

There is no light on in the bathroom, so I quickly clear it and move back out to the hallway. Making my way out to the kitchen, it's pitch black. Just when I'm about to give up, I hear a sound coming from the living room. He must be asleep on the couch. This smug son of a bitch is sleeping with ease just hours after he put hands on my one. The thought that it happened in this apartment has my blood boiling.

My heart races. It's pounding inside of my chest, and I'm pretty sure it's about to escape. Most people would hate this feeling. The nervousness. The fear. The unknown. The danger of it all. But I love it. I thrive on it. He deserves this. Let the punishment fit the crime.

And with that, I let the needle sink into his neck. The beauty in his fear when his eyes go wide with realization, it does something to me.

He jerks, but it's too late. He wants to fight, but it's too late.

My hand clamps over his mouth. My knee pins his chest down. His body convulses as the drug takes hold- first his limbs, then his chest, locking his muscles in place.

His eyes are screaming. Fear.

Scream all you want to. We can't hear you.

I lean in, close enough to feel the last bit of air leaving his lungs but not enough to kill him immediately. "Not so tough now, are you?"

He can hear everything I'm saying. He can feel every touch I give him. He will be in excruciating pain, but all he will be able to do is watch me.

Laying the tarp on the ground, I drag him on top of it and get him wrapped up like a burrito. Making sure not to suffocate him, I don't want him getting off that easily. I drag him to the back door. Opening the door, I make sure the coast is clear. Lifting with my legs I hoist him over my shoulder. "Fuck, you're heavy. Someone had one too many twinkies. Don't worry I'm not judging."

With a thud, I drop him into the bed of my truck and drive to the river edge. I've been there a few times. It's always a quiet place. Especially this time of night. He will be discovered easily by runners which is exactly what I want. I want Annabell to know he is gone. I want her to feel a peace that he can never hurt her again.

"Come on tubby," I say as I pull him out of my truck. I should probably choke the life out of him and be on my merry way, but I want to take my time with him. He deserves it.

Unwrapping him, I look deep into his eyes as I run my knife along his jaw. "You kissed her with these lips." I drag my knife over to his lips. "They have to go."

Not wasting time, I remove his lips with one swipe. "Well that's just nasty." I throw them into the water. "Goodbye pervy lips."

The tears fall from his eyes. I wish I could take my glove off and feel his tears. Touching them with my gloved finger, I smile.

"What did you touch her with next?" I give him a thinking face. "Oh, I know. Your hands. Duh."

Grabbing his hands, I cut into them. My knife isn't strong enough to break his bone so I take pleasure in stabbing them. "You should know better than to touch what isn't yours. Did your mother not teach you that? What a shame," I say as I trail the knife down to his dick. His eyes go even wider.

Yup. That's next.

"You tried to force yourself on what's mine. Tisk. Tisk. Tisk." Raising the knife up, I plunge it into him as deeply as it will go. Feeling the ground beneath me, I grin. All too soon, he passes out from the pain.

I guess my fun is over.

It's going to take him a while to bleed out, I would hate for someone to find him before he dies. I've seen way too many movies to know not to leave your victim alive.

Rectifying the situation, I slide the knife into him in the same place the syringe went in. Call it poetic justice.

Chapter 28 Conrad

Coming home to find Annabell still in my bed, had me smiling until I fell asleep. I feel like a school boy, completely obsessed with a girl... I guess it's not so far off.

Climbing into bed, I wrap my arms around her and breathe her in. I instantly get hard, but my body needs sleep. Thankfully, my dick gets the memo, and I drift off to sleep completely happy. It's a new feeling for me. I'm not used to feeling this overwhelming scene of joy. I've always been neutral. I'm not happy, but I'm also not sad.

I've always known something or someone was missing. I've always known she was the piece of my life that would change it. I've always known that as soon as I found her, my life would be whole. And I was fucking right. My life is whole with her.

Killing someone that deserved to die, coming home to wrap my arms around my girl in my bed....I'm blissfully happy, and no one will take that away from me.

I didn't know it yet, but someone would try to do just that. Someone would try to take what's mine.

My phone starts to ring, I jerk awake. My first thought is Barbara's alarm, but it's not. Someone is calling me. The name Zeak is flashing on my screen.

Why would he be calling this early?

Concern stirs in my stomach. "What's wrong?" I answer as I scoot out of bed. I don't want to leave her, but I don't want her to hear me.

"I'm not asking questions, but I was hacking into a scanner this morning…" He takes a break.

"Point Zeak?" I growl. It's too early for his early morning stories.

"I overheard someone saying they found a body out by the river today. Do I need to do damage control?" Zeak whispers the second part of the question.

Zeak knows how I like to spend my extra time. He is all for ridding the world of scum. He just doesn't have the stomach for it, so he helps me in any other way he can.

"No, that's not what I want," I almost yell. I didn't mean to. I want the body to be reported. I want Annabell to find out that he is gone. Plus, I covered my tracks well enough. There is no way it could be tied back to me.

"You got it boss. Let me know if you need me to do anything else."

"Thank's Zeak." I quickly hang up, but when I turn around I see two beautiful hazel eyes staring back at me.

"How are you feeling?" I ask as I look down at her. She has rolled over on her side to study me. She's studying me when I'm the one trying to read her.

"I'm fine. Did you bring me into your bed last night? The last thing I remember was laying on your chest," she asks. I must admit, I did enjoy having her in my bed last night. Even if all we did was cuddle.

"I did. You were upset so I brought you in here. I didn't want you to be alone." I walk over to the bed and grab her face between both of my hands. Her face feels warm. I'm not sure if it's from embarrassment or the heat of these covers, but I like it. "Are you feeling better?"

She nods her head and leans into my hands. She looks so small in my hands. It reminds me how much I need to protect her. "Did we...?" She looks up at me and asks. I can't help but laugh. That question actually came out of her mouth. It's so cute. If we had fucked, she would still feel me between her legs. I can guarantee her that.

"Why are you laughing?" Her question comes out as if she is offended by the fact I'm laughing at her.

You are too cute, Princess.

Instead of answering, I grab the covers that are covering her and rip them off. Seeing her exposed to me sends a fire through my bones. She is in my t-shirt, and fuck it looks good on her. Unable to help myself, I kneel on the bed. Making my way to her, I crawl between her legs. She opens them willingly.

Just as she should.

Crawling between her legs, I feel right. I feel at home.

I crawl to her as if I'm a lion stalking my next meal because dammit.... I want her to be my next meal. I have been craving this girl from the moment I saw her. Having to wait months to taste her has been torture.

I make my way up to her. My hands rest at either side of her head. Watching her, I gauge her reaction, and it's a good one. Her eyes start on my arms and work their way down to my chest. The moment she sees my nipple rings, her eyes go wide. I guess this is the first time she has seen me without a shirt on. Dammit, I love the way she is eye fucking me right now.

This body is all for you, Princess.

She runs her hands down my arms and over to my chest. Pausing for a moment as she looks at my piercings.

They won't bite. I may, but they won't.

Gaining some courage, she runs her finger tips over my waiting nipples. The contact causes me to tense up. My pecs contract causing my nipples to poke out more. To my desire, she seems to like the response.

Unable to wait any longer, my lips crash into hers. I've been dying to kiss her again. It was agonizing not being able to touch her like I wanted to last night. But she is here now. She is ready now, and she is willing.

My tongue enters her mouth with a force. She opens wide for me as I dive in deep. I want to swallow her whole, to make her a part of me. My hands have a mind of their own. My brain doesn't even tell my hands to move to her nipple, but it seeks it out.

Playing with her nipple, I'm met with a delicious moan. Feeling the vibration against my mouth, I match her moan. She feels so fucking good, and I'm simply kissing her.

Lost in her kiss, I feel Annabell run her hand down my chest. She doesn't stop. She is on a mission. The little siren passes go and collects her prize. Feeling her hand cup my dick, I break our kiss. Unable to stop myself, I look down. The sight of her hand on my dick almost has me blowing my load as it is.

"Fuck, Princess," I hiss. Growing impossibly harder, I watch as she dips her hand inside of my sweatpants. Watching her hand disappear, it wraps around my hard length. And I nearly lose it.

Her warm hands wrapped around my aching cock is both heaven and hell. It's heaven because…well her hand is on my dick. It's hell because I'm not inside of her. "That feels so good, Princess. You have no idea," I growl into her ear. It's taking everything I have not to rip her underwear off and have my way with her. But she deserves more than a quick fuck.

With every thrust of my hips, I imagine being inside of her. Her hand allows my dick to pass easily through it. I have a feeling her pussy isn't going to be so easy to slide into, and the thought excites me.

"I want to feel you inside of me, please," she begs. She's begging me, and I'm about to lose it like a sixteen year old boy.

You will not make a mess inside of your pants.

Leaning back on my knees, she reluctantly releases me. My eyes roam over her body. The body that I'm about to devour. The body that is forever sketched inside of my mind. It willingly lives inside of my head. There's no need to pay rent.

Running my hands down her flat stomach, I once again picture her belly swollen with my baby growing inside of her.

Soon.

Dragging my hands down both of her legs, I make my way back up to her lace panties. "While this lingerie is hot as fuck, it needs to be off of you." Grabbing the top of them, I quickly drag them down her olive toned legs.

Letting my evil side take over, I lift them to my nose and inhale the deepest breath possible. Good fucking fuck. She smells like my very own heaven.

"Oh fuck me," Annabell whimpers, interupting my thoughts.

"Oh I plan to, Princess. I plan to fuck every part of you, but I need to taste you first. That sweet smell of your arousal has me dying to lick you."

Making my way down to her sweet core, she covers her face. Why is she hiding from me?

"Don't hide from me. I want to see your eyes roll back into your head when I make you come over and over again with just my tongue," I growl at her. Her eyes are already starting to fall back into her head, and I haven't even touched her yet.

Noticing her hesitation, I pause. "What is it, Princess?"

Taking a deep breath she tells me. "I've never had anyone do this to me before. Maybe I should shower first." She makes a move to stand up.

No fucking way.

Slamming her back down onto the bed, I grab her hands and pin them above her head. How could she think she should go shower first? Does she not understand how good she smells to me? Does she not understand how badly I want to have her juices drenching my face? I guess I'll just have to show her.

"Though the thought of me being the only one to ever lick your pretty little pussy turns me on so damn much, I can't imagine who would not be on his hands and knees eating you out every night." Just the thought of running my tongue up and down her slit has me scrambling to my knees. Fuck those guys that had their chance to taste her.

She's mine now.

Cupping her warm pussy, I tease her at first. I want to see this girl squirm for me. She has no idea what's in store for her. Running my fingers down the bend of her legs, I quickly move over to trail her needy lips. Her clit is already swollen from need, and I can't wait to give it what it wants.

"Please," I hear her whisper. She's already begging me, and I've just barely touched her.

"Please what? What is it that you need so badly?" I want her to tell me exactly what she is wanting. I want to hear the dirty words coming from that pretty mouth.

"I need you on me. I need to feel your tongue. Please," she begs me again. And fuck, if it isn't the most satisfying things.

"As you wish, Princess." I grant her her first wish, but there won't only be three like a genie. There will be a lifetime of wishes granted.

Running my middle finger over her clit and down through her folds, I relish the way she responds. She bucks against me as if this is the first time she has been touched. Unable to wait any longer, I plunge my middle finger inside of her. And now it has become my favorite finger. How can my finger be receiving pleasure? It's not normal... but it's happening.

I roll my finger inside of her. Exploring every millimeter of her most private place. As far as I know... I'm the only man alive that has been inside of her. And for some reason knowing that gives me a high.

Feeling her walls start to tighten, I pull my fingers out of her. The desire takes over me. Sliding my newly favorite finger between my lips, I suck on it. Her sweet and salty taste coats my tongue.

Yup, most definitely my favorite finger.

"Now do you believe me that I am dying to taste you? So will you shut up and let me have my way with you?" She nods her head as the fire in her own eyes starts to match mine. I want this girl more than she knows, but I'm about to show her.

Spreading out on my stomach, I slide my hands between her bent legs. Looking up at her, I can't help but smile. I have my meal here. She's prepped and prepared for me. Slowly, I bend down until my face is only a half inch away from her slit. Her breathing is so ragged, I'm not sure she's going to be able to handle me waiting much longer.

Putting her suffering to an end, I roll my tongue against her clit. And it's pure ecstasy. The warmth of her covering my tongue has me going back for seconds.

"Oh yes! Please, Conrad. Please," she cries out.

The way she begs me, it pushes me on. Not that I need anything to keep me going, I'll eat her pussy on the daily if she will let me. And I have a feeling that after today she will gladly spread her legs for me.

Swirling my tongue in circles, I feel her body start to tighten. With a few more passes of my tongue, she comes apart. First, her back comes off of the bed. Then, her legs twitch uncontrollably. I never stop, not until she has completely come down from her orgasm. And what a beautiful orgasm it was. Now, to give her ten more.

As she is lost in her post orgasm high, I pull my dick out of my pants. It's been begging to come out and play. I feel like this is how I should walk around the house. Just have my dick out at all times. Let Annabell play with it anytime she wants. Fuck, that would be the life.

When her eyes open, they go wide. She watches me stroke my dick in preparation. I'm looking for any possible relief right now. My hand isn't cutting it, but knowing I'm about to sink balls deep into my new forever home, it's worth it.

Yes Princess. This is about to go inside of you.

She gives me the sweetest nod as if she is giving me permission to fuck her. Did she really think I was asking for permission? Did she really think I wasn't about to take what is mine? My evil side wants to come out to play, but sweet Annabell isn't ready for that Conrad just yet.

Lining up the tip of my dick to her hot and aching center, I'm about to push in when I hear my phone alarm going off.

No fucking way. This isn't happening right now.

Looking down, I see it's Barbara's alarms that's going off. I need to give her her medication now.

FUCK!

"Fuck. I have to go. I'm sorry, Princess." I'm pissed, but I try not to let it show. I don't want to have to deal with this broad. I want to be fucking my girl right now.

"Why do you have to go right now? Can't it wait a few minutes?" Oh she's so cute to think I would only give her a few minutes.

"I don't want just a few minutes with you. I will be taking the whole night with you. I will make you come more than you ever have. I can promise you that." Tucking myself back into my sweatpants, I look down at her. "I have a few meetings I have to get to, but I will be back for you later tonight. It will probably be late so do not go anywhere." I make sure to put an emphasis on *"do not go anywhere"*. I don't want her leaving this house.

"I will make it up to you, and you will forget all about me leaving right now," I say to her as she gives me a pouty face.

Those lips are going to look so good wrapped around my dick.

Kissing her as if it's our last kiss, I reluctantly let her go and run out of my bedroom. I know it's a risk to let her stay in my room without me there, but even if she does snoop, she won't find much. The worst thing she would find would be cash and my box of keepsakes.

Chapter 29 Conrad

Rushing down the stairs, I take the steps two at a time. Still only in my sweatpants, I'm thankful Barbara is dead to the world. My hard dick quickly fades at the thought of Barbara seeing me with no shirt on. That's not something I want to be thinking about, but it definitely helped with my raging hard-on.

Everything looks in place when I open the door to her current bedroom. She's still fast asleep. The medication is still locked in the cabinet I set in here.

"Shit, the key."

Quickly patting my pockets, I let out a breath. Relief rushes over me. I didn't lose the key when my face was buried between Annabell's legs.

Shoving the key into the lock, I grab her meds and administer them through her IV. Wanting to be in here as little as possible, I give the meds a few minutes to work. Satisfied, I leave her room and close the door behind me.

After a few hours of working, I pull up the cameras. "Are you where I left you, Princess?" I can't even get through an hour of work without thinking about her.

Flipping through the cameras, I find her in her room. "You're not supposed to be there."

I should have known she wouldn't stay put. She can't help herself.

Rewinding the feed I watch her climb onto her bed as she eats a poor excuse for breakfast. Where did she even find that breakfast bar? She turns on her new TV, and I'm pretty sure I see her smiling.

After I took care of Barbara this morning, I hooked up the new TV I bought for her. She was always watching her shows on her laptop. I could tell she enjoyed watching TV in bed. Hopefully I can watch with her soon… but we probably won't be watching for long. If I have Annabell in a bed… she's going to be naked real fast.

Pressing the live button, I see her asleep on her bed. Unable to help myself, I make my way to her bedroom.

Letting myself in, I watch as she sleeps. It's a beautiful sight. Locating her phone, I find it under her pillow. Her charge is low so I plug it in for her and set it on her bedside.

Kissing her forehead, I reach over and pet Haci. She's a great dog, always protecting and watching over Annabell.

Making my leave, I look back at my sleeping beauty. I can't believe I finally found you. And just think if I hadn't stopped and grabbed dinner at that restaurant, I might not have found you yet.

Reluctantly, I get back to work. It's been nice working from home these past couple of weeks. I've never wanted to be away from the office so much.

Of course, I have to go in when I have important meetings. Plus, it's necessary to show my face. I wouldn't let my business be jeopardized by my absence though. I'm not saying my job comes first anymore, but there has to be balance. Annabell will always come first now.

Seeing movement on my screen, I watch as my sweet Annabell rolls over. She searches for her phone. Once she finds it, I grab my phone and send her a text.

Conrad: Where are you?

Annabell: In my room. I think I might have food poisoning from an old breakfast bar.

Dammit.

Conrad: I'll be there in one minute.

Running up the stairs as fast as I can, I knock on her door. She tells me to come in, but when I open the door she is still in bed.

"Why are you eating old breakfast bars? And why did you not tell me you were sick?" I'm pissed. Does she not think she can eat anything I have in the kitchen? Hell, I'll order food for her. All she has to do is ask.

"I was starving, but didn't want to go down to the kitchen. I found it in my bag and thought it would be fine, so I ate it. I just woke up and threw up a few times. Then, I saw your text," she admits as she lays her head back down on her pillow.

Crawling into her bed, I wrap my arms around her. I hold her in silence, not wanting to disturb her. My heart is heavy. I want to be here for her. She is my priority. Everything else can wait.

    She rolls over and places her head on my chest. I can't help but smile. Feeling her against me is comforting. Even though I'm supposed to be the one rescuing her, here she is… rescuing me.

Chapter 30 Annabell

Rolling over, I find Mr. Conrad is still in my bed with me. He didn't leave. He held me most of the night, and when I was puking my guts out, he held my hair back for me. It's not the hot and heavy night I was hoping for with him, but it showed me a side of him I hadn't seen yet.

Watching him now, I can't help but feel more for him than I should. I know he's interested in me, but I don't believe it's at the same caliber as I'm feeling. He is starting to consume me, and I'm not sure I'm ready for it. But it's also all I want.

Part of me still wants to run from fear of being hurt. I know I'm going to crash when I fall. I know that because I'm not sure he is going to catch me when I do fall. But the other part of me doesn't even care.

Sneaking out of bed, I go to the bathroom to brush my teeth. I make sure to take my time and rinse with mouthwash. After puking several times last night, I really don't want to have puke breath. Gross.

When I make it back into bed, Mr. Conrad is still sleeping. I still can't get over how truly magnificent he is.

God must have sculpted him himself. And he is here with me.

Sliding back into bed, I face him. I'm still weak from being sick, but I can't help but stare at him. Leaning over, I'm overcome with the need to kiss his cheek. My lips are magnetized to his charming face. Feeling his stubble brush across my lips, it immediately makes me think of when his head was between my legs.

The movement causes him to stir. I bury my head back against the pillow, not wanting to be caught. Quickly closing my eyes, I pretend to be asleep.

Feeling movement from his side of the bed, I know he is awake and leaning towards me. "I know you're awake, Princess," he whispers into my ear.

My eyes flutter open. They are met with those dark lonely eyes that have quickly become my favorite.

Smiling at him, I'm blessed with a returned smile. He doesn't smile often, but when he does… It's magical.

"How are you feeling?" He asks as he brushes a fallen strand of hair behind my ear. The action causes both my heart and clit to swell.

"I'm feeling much better. Thank you for everything. I really didn't want you to see all of that though. It was not sexy," I admit.

Positioning himself on top of me, he spreads my legs apart. Resting his knees on the bed, he makes a squatting position. I'm assuming he does this so he isn't resting on my stomach.

That's sweet.

Placing his arms on either side of my head, he looks deep into my eyes. Our noses touch, and I want so badly to kiss him. "Do you really think I wouldn't want to take care of you?"

Meeting his intense stare, I lick my lips. His eyes dart down to my tongue. Fighting with himself, he leans down and brushes my lips with his.

I want to grab him and force him against me, but we both know I'm not ready for the kind of ride Mr. Conrad wants to give me. I'm not quite there yet, but kissing….kissing I can do.

Reaching my hands up, I grab him around the back of his head and pull him into more. Willingly, he deepens the kiss.

Feeling his tongue brush my lips, I gladly open for him. "You smell minty fresh. Did you sneak out of bed, or do you just naturally wake up like this?" He jokes with me as he kisses my neck.

"There is no way I wasn't going to sneak out of bed and brush my teeth. I couldn't put you through that," I joke back.

"Aren't you thoughtful, but I'd be kissing you this morning no matter what." His lips find their way back to mine. Pushing his tongue to the back of my throat, it's as if he is trying to taste every bit of me.

Opening my mouth impossibly wider, a moan vibrates deep in my throat. The way he is kissing me…it's like he's trying to join our mouths together. And I am here for it.

Pulling back from me, he buries his face against the crook of my neck. "I better stop, or I'm going to end up fucking you right now. And I know you're still weak," he goans into my neck.

I want this man more than anything, but he is right. I'm not feeling up to much physical activity. "Maybe we could watch a movie. Try to distract ourselves."

"Laying in bed with you, watching a movie, and not making a move on you…that's going to be very difficult," he teases me as he nips at my neck.

Looking up at him, I smile. How did I get so lucky? Even if this is temporary… I'm still incredibly lucky to have found an amazing job with the perfect guy.

"What are you thinking?" He interrupts my thoughts.

"I was just thinking how happy I am right now," I admit.

One of his rare smiles covers his morning stubble face. "You aren't even the happiest person in this room, but I'm pleased to hear that."

Sliding back to my side, he kisses the side of my head. "So what movie did you have in mind?"

After two hours of watching one of my favorite movies, my stomach growls. "Are you hungry?" Conrad asks. He hasn't left my side. It's been odd but amazing having him here with me.

He told me he took a sick day from work. Knowing he took off work just to stay home with me…I'm not sure what to think of it. I know it makes me extremely happy, but am I getting ahead of myself?

"I am. I think I'm finally ready to eat something, but no breakfast bars," I tease. Just the thought of that makes me want to puke again.

"No breakfast bars. Got it." He slides off of the bed and heads to my door.

"Where are you going?"

"To get my girl something to eat," he winks at me and walks out of the room.

My girl.

I can't stop saying it. Is that what he thinks of me? His girl? I know he said I was his, but did he really mean that?

Mine.

Twenty minutes later, he returns with two plates. Setting them down on the bed, he takes his place beside me again.

Did he make all of this for me?

There is toast, scrambled eggs, and bacon. Either he cooks really well, or he had this delivered extremely fast. "Thank you so much. This was so nice of you," I say as I stab my eggs with my fork.

I've never had someone cook me breakfast- much less bring it to me while I'm still in bed.

We eat in silence as we watch the next movie I picked out. This time I went with a romance movie I've been wanting to see. Mr. Conrad told me to pick whatever I wanted. "I'll just be watching you most of the time," he said.

There is no way I'm going to be able to focus on watching this movie. All I can think about is his body touching mine, his hands all over my skin, and his dick inside of me.

As the movie goes on, I quickly realize this isn't just a romance movie. It's extremely sexual. I've already seen three butts in three different showers, some side boobs, and now the couple is about to have sex.

Rolling my lips together, I try to keep from smiling. I'm getting turned on watching the guy take off the woman's clothes. I want to be that woman right now. Not with that guy, but with Mr. Conrad.

The guy on the screen pulls her shirt off and lowers his head to her covered boobs. He teases her with his mouth, and I can't help but look over at Mr. Conrad. And he's staring right at me. He's watching me with fire in his eyes.

Leaning over, he rubs my stomach with his hand. Sliding it under my shirt, he traces my belly button. Just the feeling of his fingers on me has my panties pooling with my arousal.

"Do you see how he is taking his time with each one of her nipples," Mr. Conrad whispers in my ear. It shocks me and causes me to jump.

Instead of speaking, I look over at him and nod my head. "Watch the movie," he orders.

Turning my head back to the screen, I watch as he pulls her jeans off. "He takes his time. Slowly exposing the place he truly desires to be in," he whispers again.

The sound of his needy voice in my ear has me wanting to pull him on top of me, but we just ate. And my stomach is still a little uneasy.

The guy pushes the girl onto the bed. He is rough as he pulls off his clothes. Making his way onto the bed, his bare ass comes into view. That's butt number four.

As he climbs between her legs, he starts to kiss her. It's a deep kiss. One that resembles the kiss Mr. Conrad and I shared this morning.

Without breaking the kiss, he pulls her bra off. Covering her left boob with his hand, he squeezes. Her moan is swallowed up by his greedy mouth.

Quickly, he pulls down her panties. You can't see it, but you can tell he slides into her. "And that's where his mistake is," Mr. Conrad growls.

Looking back over, he licks his lips. My eyes drop to them…because it's impossible not to watch his full, kissable lips.

"What mistake was that," I ask breathily.

"He didn't take enough time getting her warmed up. Sure, I'm sure she is wet for him because she wants him inside of her. But how much more pleasurable would it be for her if he slid his hands between her legs," he says as he slowly moves his hand down my stomach.

I want him between my legs so badly. I want to feel his warmth. I want to feel how much he desires me.

My chest quickly moves up and down the closer he gets to my waistband. The girl on the TV cries out as she cums. I can't help but be jealous of the on screen actress.

"You know I can make you feel a thousand times better than that. Don't be jealous of her," he says as if he is reading my mind.

Leaning over me, he gets so close to my lips. "But not right now because you need to rest." He grabs the remote from my other side and clicks the back button.

"Hey, why did you turn that off?" I lean up in bed.

"I can't have you getting all horny watching this movie. First off, I'm a little jealous. Secondly, I'm not going to be able to stop myself if you keep looking at me like that. Now, pick a different movie," he demands.

"Ugh, fine. You know, you could just slide your hands inside of my pants and feel just how horny I am," I tease him. The moment I say that, I'm shocked. His eyes almost look mad.

"It's not nice to tease, Princess. Soon, you won't be sick anymore. And I'm not going to hold back." His promise almost sounds like a threat, but I like it.

"You promise?" I tease.

"Oh I'll do more than promise….Now pick a movie," he orders.

Smiling, I select a comedy. Hopefully there aren't any sex scenes. I'm not sure I can take the teasing again. He is already irresistible. Throw in him teasing me…I'm hopeless.

"Thank you for the new TV by the way. It was really thoughtful of you."

"Of course. Anything you want, I will get it for you, Princess." His pledge makes me feel a warmth in my heart that I'm not used to. Even though our relationship might not be a forever relationship, I have no doubt in my mind that he would take care of me and my needs.

"Somehow, I believe you."

"Good! You better." Gone is the sweet man that was just promising me everything. In his place is the demanding man I have come to depend on. And I'm not sure it's a good thing.

Chapter 31 Conrad

"You can start work on Monday," I tell Annabell as soon as the ridiculous movie is over. It was supposed to be a horror movie, but it ended up just being funny.

I guess first hand experience on killing people will make Hollywood horror comical. I mean, does the damsel in distress really have to trip over the leaf in the road every time?

Annabell told me about a drinking game she played while watching a scary movie. Apparently anytime something ridiculous happened she had to drink. I'm glad to know she finds horror movies as funny as I do.

I can't help but wonder what she would think of me if she knew the real me? If she knew I killed people, but only the ones that deserve it of course. I would never hurt an innocent.

"Really? I'm so excited. Thank you." She throws her arms around me, and I breathe her in. I wish I could bottle her scent and spray it on me when she wasn't around.

"Thank you for being patient with me and not running out on me."

"I would never do that," she reassured me. God, I pray that's true. There is only so long I can keep my secrets from her at bay. One day, she will learn the truth. I just hope she accepts me when that day comes.

"So now that I'm going to be working….will I still get to see you often?" Her question makes me smile. Does she really think her starting to work with Barbara is going to change anything? It's not like she has to watch her 24/7.

"You will be spending a lot of time with me, Princess. In this bed. In my bed. On your knees. On your back. Against the wall, and anywhere else I decide to have you," I inform her. I may have come off a little too strong, but I don't care.

She clears her throat. "That sounds good to me."

"Good. I'm going to go order us some dinner, and then you're going to bed." Getting off of the bed, I stretch. I haven't sat in a bed all day long since I was a teenager. I'm stiff. And my dick hurts from being hard all day.

The rest of the night is uneventful, but it's been surprisingly great. I never thought I would spend all day with a woman and not do at least one sexual thing. Minus the kissing, we haven't done anything.

"So what exactly do you do?" She randomly asks me.

"I run a financial firm downtown," I say. Not really wanting to give her too much information just yet.

"So that's where you spend most of your time?" Does she not realize I've been here most of the time?

"I go into the office a lot, but I also have the luxury of spending a lot of time working from home."

"So you have an office here?" Her eyes light up. I guess the idea of me being home a lot makes her happy.

"I do. It's right down the hall from the garage. You can come visit me any time." I give her a wink. I'd love for her to come visit me one day. I've been daydreaming about fucking her on my desk.

"So what…." I cut her off before she can finish.

"That's enough questions for today. It's been a long day, and you need to sleep." Giving her a kiss on the cheek, I pull her into me.

"You're going to stay with me?" She's surprised I'm not leaving. Hell, I'm surprised, but I wouldn't want to be anywhere else.

"I am. Now close your eyes."

She does as she's told, and It doesn't take long before I hear the steady breathing of her slumber.

Sweet dreams, my one.

Waking to a crack of thunder, I'm shocked when I see the clock reads 2 am. I must have fallen asleep listening to her deep breathing. It was like the lullaby my mother used to sing to me. Constant. Steady. Soothing.

I can't help but think about all the ways Annabell is similar to my mother. Her hair, the same color. The way it frames her face. Her eyes, the same shade of brown. And her small frame, it's the same. But Annabell is so much more than my mother ever was.

Shaking thoughts of that woman out of my head, I slide out of bed. Though I don't want to leave her warmth and comfort, I know it will be time for me to give Barbara her medication soon. And I don't want my alarm to wake Annabell up. She needs her sleep.

After I give Barbara her medication, I make my way upstairs. Stopping in my tracks when a light comes on outside, I question who or what would be outside. Walking to the living room window, I notice it's the floodlights. They only come on when someone or something walks by.

Who the fuck is outside my house?

Small animals don't trigger the lights. Sure, it could be a deer, but what are the odds? I'm not a betting man. If I don't know the odds are in my favor, I'm not buying into it. And the odds of a deer coming up this close to the house, it doesn't sit right with me.

Grabbing my gun from my office, I throw on my shoes and make my way outside the side door. The lights are still on when I round the corner. Seeing nothing, I continue my pursuit.

Gun raised, I walk away from the house. Stepping away from the light and into the darkness, I blend into the tree line. Hiding in the shadows has always worked well for me. It's my refuge. It's my sanctuary.

The lights go off, and I'm left in complete darkness. Waiting to see if they come back on, I squat next to the large oak tree. The bark scratches my bare back, but I don't move. I just watch.

A few minutes go by, and I see nothing. Standing up, I start to make my way back to the house. As soon as I step away from the shadows of the tree, the lights come back on.

I quickly take a step back and jog down the treeline. That's when I see her. A female figure trying to hide from the bright light. She's familiar, but I can't make out her face.

Taking a few steps closer, she walks towards the side door. As soon as she steps into the light, rage floods my senses.

Fucking Rachel Evans

Why is she sneaking around my house at this time of night? She shouldn't be here regardless. I've told her several times, it's over. I don't want her showing up here where Annabell is. That would not go over well. I can't have anything screwing things up with us. She has finally let me in.

Sliding my gun between my back and my waistband, I walk out of the shadows. Rachel is peering into the window to the left of the side door.

"What the fuck are you doing here?" I basically yell. If Annabell was downstairs, she would probably hear me.

Rachel jumps at my words. Spinning to face me, she grabs her chest. "You scared the shit out of me, Conrad."

My name on her lips irritates me. She has no right to use it. She's not mine. I don't want her.

I know my thoughts are harsh, but it's how I feel. I don't want her to be around me much less to utter my name. It's for Annabell's mouth. Thinking of Annabell's mouth has my mind quickly turning in the wrong direction.

Not now Conrad.

Shaking thoughts of Annabell out of my head, I come up to Rachel. Her eyes drift to my bare chest. Her eyes drop further down to my sweatpants.

Normally, I'd enjoy a woman ogling my body the way Rachel is right now. But the only woman I want looking at me like this is my one. I'm not interested in anyone else.

"I really hate repeating myself," I growl. It's not the playful way I give Annabell. I'm pissed off.

"Oh sorry. I got distracted," she says, giving me a look that is meant to entice me…it doesn't.

"Well…?"

"I missed you, Conrad."

There she goes again, saying my name as if she owns it. The evil side of me wants to grab her tongue and tell her to never utter my name again.

Taking a deep breath in, I slowly release it. "We have been over this, Rachel. It's over between us." I try to say this as nicely as possible, but I don't think it helps.

"Why? Everything was fine. Is it because I said I was falling in love with you? I fall in love easily. Don't take it to heart. I didn't even mean for it to come out." She pauses, but I don't say anything. I'm hoping she realized I'm not going to play this little game.

"Is there someone else?" She pouts.

Instinctively, I look up at the house where Annabell is. There is this pull in me to protect her. She is my everything. I won't let Rachel ruin this.

"You need to leave. We both need some sleep," I say as I cross my arms over my chest.

"There is someone else. Isn't there? I knew it." Rachel starts pacing.

Looking closer, I notice her eyes are bloodshot. It doesn't look like she has had a good night's sleep in a long time.

"Regardless of if I have someone new, we aren't getting back together. I don't want to be harsh, but you need to get over us. We are nothing." I hope my directness is clear for her. I'm not sure what else to do.

If this doesn't sink into her head, I'm going to have to be a jerk. And I really don't feel like breaking this girl anymore than I already have.

Instead of arguing with me, she shakes her head as if I've just told her I killed her mother.

Walking backwards, she turns and runs around the house in the direction she came from.

Did she drive here?

I listen for a car starting, but I don't hear anything. How did I not see how unstable this girl was? She seemed perfectly normal when we were together. She seemed like she had potential. Now, she seems like a volcano waiting to erupt.

Chapter 32 Conrad

I've been staring at my computer for the last several hours. And it's not the fun kind where I get to watch Annabell all day. It's the kind where the boss has to play catch up on work.

Waking up in my bed this morning without Annabell wasn't how I wanted the day to go. I desperately wanted to crawl back into bed with her, but I also didn't want to wake her up at 3 A.M.

After Rachel ran off, I looked through all the outside cameras for signs of her. After she ran around the house, she ran into the woods.

Why did she come today? Why that time of night? Is she really that hung up on us?

I thought she would have been over it by now. Maybe last night got through to her. I can't imagine her not grasping it after our conversation last night. I was pretty blunt with her.

Checking my watch, I see it's already almost five in the afternoon. I can't believe I haven't seen Annabell all day. I'm surprised she hasn't come looking for me.

Pulling up the camera that's in her room, I search for her. She isn't there. Moving onto the rest of the house, I look for her like I always do. But she is nowhere to be found.

That familiar panic rushes through me. Did she go somewhere without telling me? Pulling up her phone app, I locate her phone.

"Fuck, it's inside the house," I yell. She must have left it in her room. That doesn't help me at all.

Dammit, Annabell.

Running through the whole house, I can't help but feel angst. Something isn't right.

Her bedroom is locked. Why did she lock it? Grabbing my key, I quickly unlock it. Holding my breath, I stumble into her room. It's empty, and on her bed is her phone.

Fury and fear run through me as I run back down the stairs. Shoving the side door open, I see her car is still here. I'm not sure if I'm relieved or more worried.

She's possibly still here, but I just can't find her. She could have taken an Uber somewhere. In that case, I'm going to beat her ass red. Or someone picked her up which will also earn her a nice little ass whooping.

Standing there for a moment, I think of my next move. I could check the outside cameras. I could walk around the property.

Maybe she went down to the trail I had built for her before she started working here. I hired someone to make the trail for her the moment I saw her running on the trail next to her old apartment.

Before I can decide, I hear barking in the distance. Running towards the barking, I see her dog running towards me.

She doesn't stop barking until she reaches me. "What's wrong girl? Where is your mom?" I ask her.

It's as if she knows what I ask because she turns and barks toward the trail. Every fiber in my being wants to take off down the trail to find Annabell, but I know she would want me to take care of her dog first.

Scooping her up, I run into the house, up the stairs, and into her bedroom. "Stay here. I'll go get your mom." I reassure her.

Running back outside, I take off down the trail. When I hear Annabell screaming, I pick up my pace even more.

Before I realize it, she slams into me, and I have her in my arms. She's safe now. I expect her to relax in my arms, but she doesn't. She fights against me. "No," she screams.

"Princess. I'm here. It's me." I try to reassure her, but she still thrashes against me. What is going on? What happened to her?

Grabbing her tighter, I try to comfort her. "No," she yells again as she pounds her fists into my chest.

Wrapping my arms around her, she kicks her feet. "Let me go." I fall onto the grass and roll on top of her.

"Princess. Stop. It's me. Relax. It's me." I try again, but she is lost in her fear. "Help." She calls out. Is she calling for me? Or is she scared of me? Did she find out?

"Annabell," I yell. "Annabell."

"Mr. Conrad?" Her eyes finally lock with mine, and the moment they do I see relief. Tears start to run down her face.

There's my girl. "Finally. You had me so worried, Princess. I couldn't find you. I looked everywhere for you. You were gone for so long." I wrap my arms around her and bury my face into her neck. I can't believe how scared I was that something bad happened to her.

"You're safe now," I whisper against her neck. I never want to let her go.

Her cry turns into a sob. Something must have really spooked her. Was she just terrified that she lost her dog?

"Come on. Let's get you back to the house." I scoop her up and cradle her in my arms. I hope she knows she is safe in my arms.

Once we are back inside the mansion, I set her down onto the recliner next to the sectional. She visibly relaxes, but I can tell the shock of whatever happened is getting to her.

Heading to the kitchen, I grab her a soda. "Drink this," I say once I return. I offer her the drink, but she shakes her head.

"No thanks. I don't like pop."

"This is not for your enjoyment. This is for your wellbeing. The sugar will help with the shock you're experiencing." I offer it to her again and give her an insistent look.

Thankfully, she accepts the can and takes a sip. I'm honestly surprised there was a soda can here. I wonder if Rosita left it here? If so, I'm glad she did.

"I need to look for Haci. She was gone when I woke up," Annabell says as she stands up way too quickly.

"Sit down, now." I basically yell at her. I didn't mean for it to come out quite so aggressive, but she needs to stay put.

Pushing her back onto the recliner, she relaxes again. "Haci is just fine. She found her way back to the house. It's like she was trying to rescue you."

I search her eyes for understanding. Everything is going to be alright.

I cup her face then my hand slides down to hers. "I had no idea where you were. I went outside looking for you and I saw her running towards the house barking. She was worried about you. She led me to you. Before I came for you, I put her in your room. I didn't want her to get lost."

The peace that was once in her eyes turns back to fear. "Did you see him?"

Her words are so soft I barely hear them. "See who?" My gaze narrows in on her.

There was someone out there? They are the reason for the fear in her eyes. They are the reason for the terror brought onto her. And they will be the reason I kill another person.

"There was someone out there? Is that why you were so scared?" I already know the answer, but I need her to confirm before I go too far.

"Yes," she nods.

I'm pissed. I'm having a hard time controlling my anger. I want to run outside and find whoever it was and bury them six feet under, but I can't yet. I need to make sure she is safe. They could still be out there.

"Who was it?" I finally ask. Not that I believe she will know.

"I don't know for sure. It was too dark to see." I squeeze her hand tighter. Not out of affection. It's out of anger. Not for her, but for what could have happened to her.

"Was there someone out on the trail with you?"

"Yes," she whispers. I know she's still in shock, but her one worded answers aren't helping me much. I'm tired of playing twenty questions.

"I need to check on Haci. I need to make sure she is alright." She stands up quickly, making me lean back. Standing up with her, I walk with her to the stairs. I don't want her running off, but I understand she needs to check on her dog.

"Do you have an idea of who was out there tonight, Annabell?" I'm wound so tightly I feel like I could burst at any moment, but I don't take my frustration out on her. She doesn't deserve it.

She deserves a few spankings for not telling me where she was going, but we will get to that later. Now is not the time.

"I'm honestly not 100% sure."

"Do you have any suspicions?" I know she does. I can tell by the way she answers my questions. Dammit, why doesn't she just tell me without me having to ask.

She pauses for a brief moment. Playing with her fingers, she looks up at me. "I used to have a stalker. He wasn't really harmful. All he did was talk to me a lot. He mostly just gave me the creeps. He was always around when I was outside as if he waited for me to come out. Once he grabbed my arm and scared me a little."

Even though I knew this bit of information, I'm still livid. "What?" I bark. It's almost automatic. I didn't have to pretend.

I remember watching from my truck. He put his hands on her, and I knew he had to die. I never thought he would be so daring as to come here for her.

You just sealed your fate mother fucker.

"Why haven't you told me about this guy?" I'm pissed the fuck off. Sure I know about this guy, but I don't know what he was like before I found her. I guess that's my fault for not taking care of him as soon as I saw him put a hand on what's mine.

"I never thought I needed to think about him again. I moved so I honestly thought I was done with him," she admits.

You and I both. "So you believe it was him out there?" I ask her. Trying to calm myself down, but when she doesn't answer right away my anger comes right back out.

"Annabell?" Crossing my arms, I urge her to speak. We don't have all night, and believe it or not….this is not how I wanted to spend my night.

"It could possibly be my ex-boyfriend," she nervously speaks.

This time I do have to pretend to be surprised because I knew for a fact it wasn't her ex. Unless she is referring to another ex, but I'm fairly certain she has only had one. And that mother fucker is rotting in the groud.

"Why the fuck would your ex be out here?"

After a long breath she speaks. But she doesn't tell me what I thought she would. She proceeds to tell me everything that happened the night Eric tried to force himself on her.

She tells me everything from why she went, to him trying to convince her to come back, and the details of him forcing himself on her.

My pulse is racing, but I keep my face straight. Hearing it from her lips has me reliving everything over. I wish he was still alive so I could cut off his pervy lips again. I should have taken more time with him. Now that I see the pain in her eye, I know he deserved so much more.

But I need to deal with this stalker of hers, and I know just where to find him. And unlike Eric's place- his area is a shit hole. No one is going to come looking for him. No one is going to be watching. No one will even care if I drag this dead body out for display. Just another reason Eric deserved to die. Letting my Annabell live in a shit hole like that…it's messed up.

"I want you to go up to your room and lock your door. I will be right back. Do not come outside for any reason. Do you understand, Annabell?"

I sure hope she listens to what I'm saying. No, I don't think he is still out there, but if he is…I don't want her being a witness to what I'm about to do to him.

"Yes Sir," she says as she turns and walks upstairs. Every ounce of me wants to follow her upstairs and show her the comfort she truly needs. One that will let her know I'm here for her. One that goes deeper than just a presence.

Before I march into her bedroom, I run down the stairs. I need to make sure the perimeter is clear. I may not have police or military training, but I've taken Taekwondo since a very young age. My father wanted me to be able to take care of anyone that got in my way. I wish I could thank him for that.

Grabbing the gun from my locked desk drawer inside of my office, I make my way outside. Jogging down the trail where I found Annabell, I crouch down and listen. Instead of hearing someone like I hoped, I only hear the storm rolling in.

I want to go after whoever it is, but the storm coming in is going to prevent me from hearing anyone. They could still be out here waiting, or they could have run home.

Annabell thinks it was either Eric or her stalker, Tod. We can obviously rule out Eric being as he is eating worms. Unless he has risen from the grave.

Pissed off that this storm is going to mess up my chances of tracking down whoever was out there, I run back to the mansion. I will deal with Tod tomorrow and I cannot wait.

Chapter 33 Conrad

"Coast is clear, but you are staying with me tonight," I say to Annabell as I usher into my bedroom. There is no way she is leaving my side tonight.

After finding her on the staircase wandering around, I searched her bedroom. She was scared someone was in her room because her door was unlocked. I guess I didn't lock it back when I was in a hurry to find her.

I hate that I caused her more fear, but I couldn't very well tell her it was me that went into her room. I'll come clean one day, but today is not that day.

Her dog follows us into my room just before I shut the door and lock it. I made sure all the exterior doors and windows are locked, and I doubt anyone will break in. But I'm not playing with her life. I can't lose this one.

Walking over to my chest of drawers, I pull out a clean T-shirt. "Here, put this on." Once I hand it to her, I sit on the bed. She seems nervous, and I'm not sure why.

"If you feel more comfortable, you can change in the bathroom," I offer. I really don't want her to hide herself from me, but I would understand if she needed some privacy tonight.

Instead of walking off to the bathroom like I expect her to, she turns around and pulls off her tight top. Letting it fall to the floor, she turns back and looks at me.

Her eyes fall to mine, and I can't help but feel desire for her. She's standing topless in front of me, and it's taking all of my control not to spin her around and suck on her bare nipples.

Pulling on my shirt over her head, she turns around once she is fully covered. Facing me once again, she kicks off her shoes and socks. Seeing the release in her eyes, it brings me some comfort.

My eyes can't leave her. Even if I wanted them to. I watch her as if I'm waiting for her to break. She's my porcelain doll. I want to keep her on my shelf, safe from the outside world.

Still watching every movement, she pulls off her leggings and steps out of them. Instead of crawling into bed, she sways over to me.

My shirt looks like a short dress on her, and she has never looked sexier. This should be her work attire, though I'd never get anything accomplished other than making her cum.

My fingers itch to touch her, to slide my hands under that shirt. I want to feel her. I want to make her tremble for a new reason. Not because she is scared, but because she is so turned on she can no longer take it.

"Do you mind if I take a shower?" She asks me through hooded eyes. If I didn't know any better…I'd say she was turned on. I want to say, *"only if I can join,"* but I don't.

"Of course. Come on. I will grab you a washcloth and a towel." Leading her into the bathroom, I hand her the towel.

Stepping inside the shower, I place the washcloth on the railing and turn on the shower. It doesn't take long for the shower to heat up, but I want it to be nice and warm for her.

When I exit the shower, I grab onto her waist. Just a moment to touch her. A moment to feel what's mine. A moment to know this is real and she is safe with me.

Just as I'm about to leave, she holds my stare. I can tell she doesn't want me to go. "Will you join me?"

I literally almost blurt out, *"fuck yes,"* but I don't thankfully. "Yes."

My voice sounds raspy. It sounds like my throat is dry, but it's really just because I'm turned on as fuck. I mean…how could I not be. Look at her. Just in a T-shirt, hair a mess, vulnerable.

Not wasting any time, I reach down and grab the hem of the shirt. Pulling it over her head, I leave her standing there naked.

She's breathtaking. Not only do I want to fuck this girl so bad…I want to mark her as mine. I want to mark her every way possible. I want to put her on a pedestal so no one questions how important she is to me.

Eyeing her up and down, I step back so I can take all of her in. From her beautiful rosy cheeks, to her matching tits, down to her beautiful stomach that will house our children. She is utterly perfect.

Watching her sway back and forth, I know she is nervous. Here I am fully clothed watching her as she is completely naked. It's the epitome of vulnerability, and I love it.

Seeing her bare to me has me immediately hard. There was no semi erection. I went from soft to stone hard. She does it to me everytime, and I don't see things changing.

Ready to feel her naked skin against mine, I pull my shirt over my head and throw it into the hamper. Watching her eyes drop to my chest, I slowly unbutton my jeans. It's unbearably slow, but I love watching her squirm.

My jeans fall from my waist incredibly slowly. It's like molasses dripping from a spoon. I can tell she is growing impatient; it makes me smile.

Stepping out of my jeans, I leave them on the floor. It usually drives me crazy to leave a mess anywhere, but I will pick them up later.

Hooking my thumbs inside of my briefs, I pull them down much faster. My dick springs free. It bounces up and down, and she watches every movement.

Unable to wait any longer, I pull us both into the shower. The moment the water hits my back, I relax into it. I didn't realize how much tension I was holding onto. The only better release would be to spill into Annabell right now.

Backing into me, her body is pressed firmly against me. She wants me close, and I silently thank her for that. Rubbing my hands up and down her arms, she leans her head against my chest.

Wrapping my hand around her neck gently, I bend down to her ear. "My Princess."

"My Prince," she whispers back at me. I love the endearment, but I'm nobody's prince…well maybe I could be hers.

"For you, I will be your prince. I will also be your evil. I will always protect you, Annabell. I will quite literally do anything for you." My hand lowers to her stomach.

Drawing circles I continue my promise. "If anyone tries to hurt you, they won't live to see another day. It is my purpose to keep you safe. It is my desire to see you happy, and I plan to do everything I can to make that happen. Even if that means removing people from this earth."

I hope my words don't scare her off. I'm tired of holding back. I want her to know just how much she means to me. I want her to understand the lengths I would go to to keep her safe. Hell, I've already gone to great lengths to keep her safe. And I will do it again and again.

"You are mine, Princess. No one else will ever take you from me. No one will even come close to trying. I will end every life that tries to come between us. Do you understand?"

Her breathing picks up, but I don't think it's out of fear. "Yes, I understand."

Those three words are a promise of themselves. She understands…or at least she will.

Grabbing the washcloth, I wash her slowly. Enjoying every part of her. I want to memorize every feature, every freckle, every scar, every part of her that makes her her.

With every pass of the washcloth, I ache even more. I ache for her. I ache because of her. I need to be inside of her for the first time. Finally, I need her.

When I finish torturing myself…I mean washing her…I start to wash myself. My eyes never leave hers. She watches as I rub my arms and abs, as my muscles flex and relax.

Taking the washcloth from me, she takes control. "Please sit down. It's my turn to take care of you."

Usually I'm not one to give up control, but I want to see where this goes. I want to give her what she desires, so I back up and take a seat.

The tile seat is cold and causes me to tense up, but watching her quickly warms me up. Meeting her eyes, I wait for her next move.

I want to grab her and have my way with her, but I'm also enjoying the show. Her standing there with soap running down her naked body, fuck.

Instead of washing me with the washcloth, she tosses it aside. The action causes me to grin. My evil girl has come out to play, and I love it.

Squirting soap onto her hands, she lathers them up. Starting at my shoulders, she makes her way down my arms and over to my chest. Playing with my piercings, she smiles.

"I am in absolute love with these," she says as she bites her lip.

"Good because they're all for you." Because they literally are. She doesn't know that I got these to represent finally finding her after so long. I'll tell her one day.

She washes every inch of me that she can reach. Every inch that is besides my throbbing dick. It's been staring her in the face this whole time. Begging her to give it some attention, but she doesn't.

Kneeling on the floor, she washes my legs. Just seeing her in this position, on her knees...for me, it's driving me insane. I'm at my breaking point. I'm either going to have to be inside of her or get out of this damn shower.

Thinking she is done, she surprises by climbing on top of my lap.

Fuck me.

I can't handle this. Her heat brushes against my dick and it takes every minute ounce of power in me not to grab her hips and thrust inside of her.

But then she raises up. My dick automatically lines up with her entrance. I'm praying to the God above.

Please lower yourself onto me.

And by some miracle, my prayer is answered. That's exactly what she does. As soon my dick breaks through her wet folds, I forget my own name. I forget about everything in my life. I forget to breathe. Hell, I don't even remember how to breathe. I forget what brought us here. The only thing I remember...is her.

We are connected. It's the way we should have always been connected. I can feel my world changing. It's as if I'm in a sci-fi movie and our souls are joining because they quite literally are. No one will ever be able to rip us apart.

I thought the moment I saw her was life altering. It's nothing compared to this moment. It's not just the best sex, and I can't wait to get off. It's an earthquake in my body. It's uniting. It's two people merging into one. This girl is cemented in me, and she can't be removed.

"Fuck, Princess." I can't form any other words at this moment. I'm begging myself to take it slow. Literally pleading with the evil inside of me not to ruin this moment, but I'm losing my grip. My head is spinning, and I can't tell my reality.

"Conrad," she moans into my ear and the evil side wins. I hold her in place, I push deeper inside of her. Slamming into her, my hips buck off of the tile seat. If I'm not careful I might break the seat, but I don't care. It would absolutely be worth it.

She holds onto me for dear life. The beast has been released and there is no stopping him now. My hips move faster and faster as if I'm trying to cross a finish line that doesn't exist.

Fuck, I wish it didn't exist. I could stay inside of her, buried deep all day. To feel her bare to me. To feel her come apart for me over and over. I want nothing more.

I have waited for this for what feels like multiple lifetimes. I'm not going back now. Never. She's fucking MINE.

My lips latch onto her neck and chest. Every part of her that my mouth can reach, it does. It's all too happy to oblige. My mouth can't get enough.

Then, her lips are on mine. I'm not even sure how they got there, but I'm overjoyed when I feel them. Her lips are a sweet treat to my mouth, and I devour them.

She sucks on my lower lip, and I can't help but think how good her lips would feel wrapped around my dick.

Breaking away for a moment to catch my breath, I tell her where my mind just went. "I can't wait for those lips to be wrapped around my dick, Princess."

"Mmm," she moans as I dig my fingers into her.

I can't get enough of her. I want more even though I'm still buried deep inside of her. She has changed me…and I'm not so sure it's for the good. Don't get me wrong, I'm so happy to have her…but I have a feeling I'll never be satisfied. I'll always want more and more of her.

She is my yin to my yang, and I can't be more thankful to be simply touching her . But the darkness wants to take over. It wants to cloud my judgment. I want to pull her into the shadows with me where she can't escape because she's mine. And she will forever be mine.

Feeling her start to tighten around me, I continue my assault on her body. My length slipping out just a little and slamming back into her as far as it will go. A loud moan breaks from her lips.

Her head leans back and her orgasm erupts like a volcano. Picking up my speed, so I can ride her orgasm out with her, I do the same.

My cum spills into her, coating her with it. I feel her entire body go limp just as I moan my release. It's the best orgasm I've ever had. I knew it would be. I knew everything with her would be earth shattering.

Did she just pass out? Fuck.

I've never had that happen to me before. I guess it's safe to say…she put everything she had into that. I'd like to think it's because I gave her a life changing orgasm. I plan to do that for her every night. She has no idea.

Carrying her to the bed, I dry her off the best I can before covering her with the thick comforter. Drying myself off, I climb into bed with her after I turn the shower off.

Seeing her eyes flutter open, she smiles. "You are mine, Princess. You will always and forever be mine," I whisper against her neck as she starts to drift off again. Not expecting her to respond, I kiss her on the forehead and lay my head next to hers.

"I am," I think I hear her say, but I can't be sure as it was almost inaudible.

After a few moments I only hear her deep breathing as I hold her against me. I've never been able to sleep like this. I'm not one for cuddling while I'm trying to sleep, but with her I don't feel the urge to escape. I've always needed my space, but with her it's different. Everything about her is different. She's my one, and I'm hers.

Leaning down to kiss her temple, I whisper into her ear. "I'll never let anything bad happen to you, Princess." And I mean it. I've never meant something more in my life. I mean it with every fiber in my body.

The only thing is….I didn't know it at the moment, but not all promises can be kept just because you mean them.

Epilogue- Anonymous

I watch you. I wait for you. I hate you, Annabell Brown.

You think you're better than me with the way you walk around the house. The way you talk to people in that sweet voice of yours. It's all a lie. It's all a facade.

You pretend to be better than people with the way you dress. You try to get people's attention with the clothes you wear. You want attention. Well, I'm here giving it to you. You just don't know it yet.

The way you took over like that… it's not right. It's not fair, and it won't last. You won't be in this position long. You will be out on the streets soon.

He doesn't want you. He doesn't want anyone for long. I know the way he treats women. They go in and they come out like a revolving door. You're just another toy he will use and toss away when he is finished with you. Don't get your hopes up poor girl.

I've been watching you for longer than you know. I know who you are, but you don't know me. Not yet anyways. But you will soon enough.

You think you're safe in that house? If only you knew how many times I've broken in and watched you sleep. How many times I've touched your clothes and your things.

You wouldn't be cuddled up with him if you knew what I knew. If you knew him the way I know him. The things I've done for him... or to him.

Take it in while you can, poor girl. The darkness is coming, and you won't be able to escape unscathed. I can promise you that.

I watch you. I wait for you. I hate you. You must die, Annabell Brown. Darkness is upon you.

ABOUT THE AUTHOR

Mom
Book Obsessed
TV Binger
Dog Lover
Foodie
Often lost in my other life that is writing…it's where the magic happens.

Learn more about Dahlia Dempsey and follow her on facebook for giveaways, teasers, and new releases.
authordahliadempsey@gmail.com

Visit her website at:
dahliadempsey.com
Tiktok: @dahlia.dempsey.author
Instagram: @dahlia.dempsey.author

📚**Other Books by Dahlia Dempsey**📚

Our Time

💕 Romance
👤 Single Dad + Single Mom
🖤 Slow burn
📚 forced proximity
🌶 spice
🚫 Forbidden Love
🤪 Reversed age gap

Love and Work

💨 Rom Com
👫 Friends to Lovers
🎁 Why Choose- at first
👫 Close Proximity
📚 Office Romance
🌶 SPICE spice baby
🌐 MFM

My Evil- Book 1

😼 Age Gap
🖤 He Falls First
😶 Secrets
👫 Forced Proximity
🌶 Spice
🍃 Opposite Attract
🔮 Twist Ending

Special Thanks.

I want to thank all of my Beta and ARC readers. You all made this much easier for me.

To my beloved PA, Britney Oliver: You freaking ROCK! You are going to do great things.

To my author group: You all have given me so much support. I couldn't ask for more.

Last but not least: Thank you to Mandie DeVito for helping me edit my book. We all know how great I am with edits.

www.ingramcontent.com/pod-product-compliance
Lightning Source LLC
LaVergne TN
LVHW011947060526
838201LV00061B/4235